SCIENCE BEHIND SPORTS

Skiing

TITLES IN THIS SERIES INCLUDE:

Baseball

Basketball

Car Racing

Cycling

Equestrian

Figure Skating

Football

Golf

Gymnastics

Ice Hockey

Skiing

Snowboarding

Soccer

Surfing

Swimming

Volleyball

Wrestling

SCIENCE BEHIND SPORTS

Skiing

MELISSA ABRAMOVITZ

LUCENT BOOKS
A part of Gale, Cengage Learning

GALE
CENGAGE Learning

Farmington Hills, Mich • San Francisco • New York • Waterville, Maine
Meriden, Conn • Mason, Ohio • Chicago

GALE
CENGAGE Learning®

LIBRARY OF CONGRESS CATALOGING-IN-PUBLICATION DATA

Abramovitz, Melissa, 1954-
Skiing / by Melissa Abramovitz.
pages cm. -- (Science behind sports)
Summary: "Lucent Books' "Science Behind Sports" Series explores the scientific principles behind some of the most popular team and individual sports, such as baseball, hockey, gymnastics, wrestling, swimming, and skiing. Each volume in the series focuses on one sport and opens with a brief look at the featured sport's origins, history and changes to rules, equipment, or techniques. Subsequent chapters cover the biomechanics and physiology of playing, related health and medical concerns, and the causes and treatment of sports-related injuries"-- Provided by publisher.
Includes bibliographical references and index.
ISBN 978-1-4205-1155-0 (hardback)
1. Skis and skiing--Juvenile literature. 2. Sports sciences--Juvenile literature.
GV854.315.A27 2014
796.93--dc23
2014003802

Lucent Books
27500 Drake Rd
Farmington Hills MI 48331

ISBN-13: 978-1-4205-1155-0
ISBN-10: 1-4205-1155-6

Printed in the United States of America
1 2 3 4 5 6 7 18 17 16 15 14

CONTENTS

FOREWORD

On March 21, 1970, Slovenian ski jumper Vinko Bogataj took a terrible fall while competing at the Ski-Flying World Championships in Oberstdorf, West Germany. Bogataj's pinwheeling crash was caught on tape by an ABC *Wide World of Sports* film crew and eventually became synonymous with "the agony of defeat" in competitive sporting. While many viewers were transfixed by the severity of Bogataj's accident, most were not aware of the biomechanical and environmental elements behind the skier's fall—heavy snow and wind conditions that made the ramp too fast and Bogataj's inability to maintain his center of gravity and slow himself down. Bogataj's accident illustrates that, no matter how mentally and physically prepared an athlete may be, scientific principles—such as momentum, gravity, friction, and aerodynamics—always have an impact on performance.

Lucent Books' Science Behind Sports series explores these and many more scientific principles behind some of the most popular team and individual sports, including baseball, hockey, gymnastics, wrestling, swimming, and skiing. Each volume in the series focuses on one sport or group of related sports. The volumes open with a brief look at the featured sport's origins, history, and changes, then move on to cover the biomechanics and physiology of playing, related health and medical concerns, and the causes and treatment of sports-related injuries.

In addition to learning about the arc behind a curve ball, the impact of centripetal force on a figure skater, or how water buoyancy helps swimmers, Science Behind Sports readers will also learn how exercise, training, warming up, and diet and nutrition directly relate to peak performance and enjoyment of the sport. Volumes may also cover why certain sports are popular, how sports function in the business world, and which hot sporting issues—sports doping and cheating, for example—are in the news.

Basic physical science concepts, such as acceleration, kinetics, torque, and velocity, are explained in an engaging and accessible manner. The full-color text is augmented by fact boxes, sidebars, photos, and detailed diagrams, charts, and graphs. In addition, a subject-specific glossary, bibliography, and index provide further tools for researching the sports and concepts discussed throughout Science Behind Sports.

CHAPTER 1

The History of Skiing

Skiing has existed for thousands of years, starting out as a means of transportation through snow and evolving to become a popular recreational and competitive sport. Skis originated during the Stone Age more than twenty thousand years ago and are among the oldest human tools still in use. According to the book *Two Planks and a Passion,* "The ski is even older than the wheel. . . . The ski is one of the few Stone Age implements handed down to us in their original form."1 During the last Ice Age, which began about twenty-two thousand years ago, snow up to a mile deep covered Greenland, Northern Europe, and much of North America. Historians believe our Cro-Magnon human ancestors living in Northern Europe at this time first built skis to get around and hunt for food in the deep snow.

Archaeologists have found ancient cave and rock drawings and carvings in Northern Europe that show hunters on skis chasing wild animals. The word ski, in fact, comes from the Norwegian word *skió,* which means stick of wood. Most of the artifacts archaeologists found are 4,000 to 6,000 years old, though some are older. The oldest ski ever found was discovered near Moscow, Russia, in the 1960s. Made of wood, the broken ski is about 8,000 years old. Most of the other ancient skis discovered by archaeologists have been located in Scandinavia. One of the best-known is the 5,500-year-old Kalvtraskskidan ski found in Sweden in 1924 near the village of Kalvtrask. This ski and a variety of others indicate that ancient people used different types of skis for different snow conditions, as skiers do today. They used short, wide skis in loose, deep snow and long, narrow skis on hard-packed snow.

FRESH POWDER

People in Scandinavia have been skiing for thousands of years. Norwegians have a popular saying that they are born with skis attached to their feet.

Keeping in Touch and More

The primary use of skis for transportation continued for many centuries, and gradually people began using skis to get places for purposes other than hunting. The Holmenkollen Oslo Ski Museum in Norway explains, "Skis were necessary tools in the old farming communities. High mountains, deep fjords and large plateaux were natural obstacles to communication during the winter time. Skis were therefore an important way for people to maintain contact with each other."[2] A book written by the Norwegian writer Egil Skallagrimsson around 950 A.D. describes how King Haakon of Norway devised another use for skis—he started sending his tax collectors out on skis to do their job. Mail delivery on skis also began around this time.

Although skiing for recreation and competition did not become popular for many centuries, there is evidence that skiers discovered the fun, sport-related qualities of sliding quickly through snow far earlier than recreational and competitive skiing became widespread. History books describe ski races occurring as early as 500 A.D. Writings by the ancient Greek historian Procopius, for example, "described gliding Finns (apparently using what we might recognize as skis) racing nongliding Finns (apparently using what we might recognize as snowshoes),"[3] states the book *The Physics*

Anatomy of a Ski

Although they come in many varieties, modern skis share several basic parts. The upturned front of the ski is called the tip, and the back of the ski is known as the tail. Tails can be flat or upturned, depending on the skier's needs. The skis of skiers who do acrobatics in the air, for instance, often have upturned tails to stabilize the skiers' landings, much like airplane wing flaps do. Between the tip and tail is the ski's middle, or waist. Most modern skis are shaped so that the middle is higher than the tip and tail. This quality is known as camber. The amount of camber changes when the skier's weight shifts during turns and other movements, and the stiffness of different types of skis is responsible for how much the camber changes. For example, cross-country skis are stiffer than Alpine skis, so their camber does not change as much when a skier stands and moves on them. Some modern skis known as rockers are designed with reverse camber to facilitate skiing in deep, loose snow.

of Skiing. Ski competitions were also documented around 1000 A.D. in stories about how the Viking king Harald Hadrade participated in ski racing and in betting on ski races.

In the 1300s, Scandinavian armies began sending soldiers out to fight on skis, and the first-documented skiing competitions for soldiers took place in the 1700s. In 1843, the first public, nonmilitary skiing competition was held in Tromso, Norway. After that, skiing for recreation and competition became popular for people of all ages.

New Innovations

One factor that spurred the popularity of recreational and competitive skiing was the beginning of downhill skiing. The earliest type of skiing was cross-country skiing, which is mostly done on flat or non-steep surfaces. By examining ancient skis, archaeologists determined that the bindings (the parts of skis that anchor them to the skier's boots) were loose and flexible. Loose bindings cannot be used for skiing down steep hills because they do not hold the boots tightly enough. Downhill skiing on steep hills began only after the Norwegian skier Sondre Norheim constructed the first stiff bindings out of birch wood in 1850. This type of skiing quickly became popular as a fun and exhilarating sport.

Norheim also invented the curved skis that are similar to modern skis, and he helped pioneer the sport of ski jumping. For these innovations, and because he won the first national skiing competition in Norway in 1868, Norheim is known as the father of modern skiing.

A history article about Norheim reveals that one inspiration for his development of ski jumping was simply watching Norwegian families add their own twists and turns to basic everyday skiing: "A popular activity on Sundays was to come together and have a joyful time on the slopes and hills. Some were eager to surpass each other in the most spectacular skiing acrobatics—like jumping from the roofs."[4]

Across the World

Meanwhile, as the sport of skiing was branching out in Europe, it was also gaining traction in North America. Historians believe that skis originally were brought to North America ten thousand to twenty thousand years ago by

A skier glides down a ski jump hill in the 1900s. Ski jumping as a competitive sport began in Norway in the late nineteenth and early twentieth centuries.

Skiing was a popular pastime in the United States by 1925, the year this photo was taken in New York City.

Europeans who first migrated to Asia, and then crossed to America via a land bridge that once joined Siberia with Alaska. These settlers (the Native American Indians) also brought snowshoes, and for many centuries used the snowshoes rather than skis because they found snowshoes better suited to the deep, loose snow in the areas where they lived. When European colonists later came to North America in the 1500s and 1600s, they reported that the Native Americans used snowshoes woven from animal skins.

The first written mention of skis being used in the United States appeared in the 1800s after Scandinavian immigrants introduced the sport of skiing to the Northeast. As American settlers moved westward in the 1870s and 1880s, people in mining communities in the Rocky Mountains began using skis for transportation and mail delivery in winter after discovering that skis were more efficient than snowshoes in that area. Recreational skiing gradually became popular out west as well, and in the 1900s Northern European immigrants started opening skiing schools throughout the United States and Canada. Different schools emphasized different styles of skiing from countries such as Austria, Norway, France, and Switzerland.

Today, skiing schools throughout the world offer instruction in many different skiing styles, but these styles all fall under the major categories of Alpine, Telemark, adventure, and freestyle. Although these types of skiing vary considerably, they all employ similar basic equipment: two skis, two poles, boots, and bindings. Some people consider related sports, such as monoskiing and snowboarding, which use a single ski or board, to be forms of skiing, but skiing experts say they are different sports.

Alpine Skiing

Alpine, or downhill skiing, is the most popular type of skiing today. According to the book *World of Sports Science,* "Alpine skiing includes all forms of the sport that involve skiing in mountain settings; the Alpine classification is derived from the Alps mountains of south central Europe where this form of skiing originated."[5] Most ski resorts throughout the world primarily cater to recreational and competitive Alpine skiers, and World Cup and Olympic Alpine events are among the most widely viewed competitive sports. Alpine skiing has been an Olympic sport since 1936, with medals awarded for the fastest time down a set course in five events—the downhill, slalom, giant slalom, super giant slalom (super-G), and Alpine combined. An offshoot of Alpine skiing called speed skiing is not an Olympic sport, but is the fastest nonmotorized sport in the world. Speed skiers hurtle straight down mountains instead of making turns the way most Alpine skiers do, achieving speeds of more than 150 miles per hour (241.4kph), compared to 90 miles per hour (144.8kph) for elite Alpine skiers.

The downhill is the fastest Olympic Alpine event, consisting of one race on a course that includes straight stretches, turns, hills, valleys, and bumps. Participants enjoy the thrill of speeding down steep slopes, though the danger of serious injuries from falling off mountains increases with increasing speed.

Downhill courses contain gates, but these gates only serve to help skiers stay on the course. In contrast, in slalom events, a series of closely spaced gates forces skiers to weave in and out using very tight turns. Ski gates are not like gates that swing open and closed. Ski gates consist of two long, vertical poles. Skiers ski in between these poles.

Franz Pfnuer participates in the Alpine combined slalom at the 1936 Olympic Games, the first to include Alpine skiing.

Ski Lifts

Skiers used to climb up hills to ski down in downhill skiing, but nowadays a ski lift takes them to the top. There are several types of ski lifts. Aerial lifts are most commonly used. Some aerial lifts contain a series of chairs or benches hooked up to a system of engine-driven cables attached to long poles. Others use enclosed trams or gondola cars attached to motorized cables.

Less commonly used are surface lifts. Most of these are essentially conveyor belts that transport skiers while they are standing up or sitting down with their skis in contact with the snow. One surface lift, the J-bar, has J-shaped metal tubes hanging from wire ropes. The skier sits on part of the J-tubes. A similar lift is called the T-bar. Both are said to be uncomfortable and are rarely used today. Another type of surface lift, called the Poma lift, is widely used in Europe, but not in the United States. A Poma lift contains metal bars attached to cable wires and a pulley system of levers. Skiers sit on a plastic disk at the bottom of the bars with a stick between their legs. They hold on to handgrips to stay balanced. An operator pulls the levers, which activate the pulleys that drag the skiers up the mountain.

The word slalom comes from the Norwegian words *sla* (meaning slanted terrain) and *lảm* (meaning traces in the snow). Slalom skiers run the course twice, and their times from each run are added together to determine the winner. The regular slalom is the shortest Alpine event and technically the most difficult because the gates are placed so close to one another that the skier is constantly turning at high speeds. The skier is allowed to touch but not straddle the gates, and missing a turn around a gate disqualifies the skier. In order to maintain control of the fast turns, slalom skiers use shorter skis than those used by downhill skiers.

The gates in the giant slalom and super-G are not as close together as those in the regular slalom, so skiers can go faster because they are not constantly turning. Elite super-G skiers can reach speeds of up to 60 miles per hour (96.5kph).

In the final type of Alpine event, the Alpine combined, each skier runs a combination of courses. In the Olympic Alpine combined, for example, each skier does one downhill and two slalom runs.

Birger Ruud competes in ski jumping at the 1936 Olympics. The Games have had a ski jumping category since 1924.

Telemark Skiing

All types of Alpine skiers use fixed bindings that attach their boots to the skis at both the heel and toe. This keeps the boots affixed to the skis during steep downhill runs. Fixed bindings release the boot only if the skier falls hard. Cross-country skiers, on the other hand, require free-heel, hinged bindings to allow skiers to climb hills and turn in all types of snow during long-distance runs over varied terrain. Free-heel bindings let the feet move to make these actions possible. An article in the 1935 *Canadian Ski Year Book* explains: "To telemark to the left, advance the right foot until the turnup of the back ski rests against the ankle of the right or forward foot. . . . Both knees will be well bent and the heel of the back foot will be up off the ski."[6]

All types of skiing that use free-heel bindings are categorized as Telemark skiing, and cross-country (also referred to as Nordic) skiing is the most popular type of Telemark skiing. Cross-country has been an Olympic sport since 1924 for men and since 1952 for women. Racecourses range from 6 to 31 miles (10 to 50km). Ski jumping, which is an offshoot of Nordic skiing, and Nordic combined, which consists of both cross-country and ski jumping events, have been men's Olympic sports since 1924 as well. Female ski jumping finally made its debut at the 2014 Winter Olympics in Sochi, Russia.

In ski jumping competitions, skiers jump from one specially constructed hill, fly through the air, and land on a smaller hill. Olympic ski jumping competitions include one team and two individual events. These are the normal hill, large hill, and team large hill. A separate event called ski flying takes place in some competitions that are held at one of the few ski flying hills in the world. Ski flying is just like ski jumping, but the skiers fly farther.

Ski jumpers are expected to fly a distance known as the

Ski Equipment Qualities

Skiers can choose from a wide variety of skis and other equipment, depending on personal characteristics and the type of skiing they do. In general, however, shorter, more flexible skis are best for beginners, while stiffer, longer skis are faster, so more experienced skiers tend to favor them. Most beginners use chin-high skis and most elite skiers use skis that are forehead-high. Also, in general, Alpine skis tend to be shorter and wider and have more of a sidecut than skis used with free-heel bindings. Slalom skis have the deepest sidecuts of all, because this helps skiers control the tight turns involved in slalom skiing.

Other ski equipment is also available to suit a skier's individual needs. Ski poles come in a variety of lengths and have a variety of handgrips. Adventure skiers tend to use poles with adjustable lengths so they can vary the length to meet different snow conditions and to accommodate uphill or downhill travel. Freestyle skiers tend to use short poles that will not get in the way during acrobatics.

Ski boots come in many shapes and sizes, too. Wearing comfortable, well-fitted boots is extremely important, both for preventing blisters and numbness in the feet and for properly positioning the feet to transfer energy from the skier to the skis. Boots that fit poorly prevent skiers from staying balanced and performing well, so many skiers choose to buy custom-made boots.

FRESH POWDER

Over 90 mph (144.8kph)

Speeds competitive downhill skiers can reach on a slope—faster than cars on highways.

K-point in each event. Scores for how far each jump exceeds or falls short of the K-point are combined with points for style to determine the winners. In team events, four jumpers each jump twice and the combined highest team score wins.

Other Types of Skiing

The other main types of skiing, adventure and freestyle, grew out of Alpine and Nordic skiing and combine elements of each. Adventure skiing began in the late 1800s in Europe with ski touring, which involved skiers going from ski hut to ski hut, after new types of bindings made both downhill and cross-country skiing possible. These skiers used bindings that could be switched from free-heel to heel-bound, depending on the terrain.

Today, adventure skiing, also known as backcountry skiing, refers to skiing performed outside of resorts or organized ski courses. "Backcountry skiing lets you step outside of the lines to make your own tracks in the snow,"[7] states the book *Cross-Country Skiing: Building Skills for Fun and Fitness*. Much like backpackers, backcountry skiers must be proficient in survival skills as well as in skiing techniques, as they are faced with unpredictable weather and snow conditions. They carry survival equipment such as shovels, tarps, and blankets in case they are stuck outdoors overnight, and they learn to dig snow pits or caves to help them survive under adverse conditions.

Just as adventure skiing pushes the limits of skiing as a structured sport, freestyle skiing began as a less-structured form of competitive skiing in the 1930s, when several Norwegian Alpine and Nordic skiers started doing acrobatics and other tricks to show off and entertain spectators. These tricks evolved into two main types of freestyle skiing—moguls and aerials. In moguls, steep courses are set up with multiple bumps and valleys, and skiers execute a series of jumps, twists, flips, and other movements as they

descend the course. Points are awarded for speed and complexity. In aerials, skiers leap from a ramp on a very steep hill while performing acrobatics in the air. Competitors often take off at speeds of around 60 miles per hour (100kph) and jump more than 50 feet (15m) upward while doing numerous gymnastics-like tricks. They then land on another hill, and judges award points for difficulty, technique, and the quality of the landing.

At first, freestyle skiers were viewed as lunatics jumping off cliffs, and the sport was classified only as an "extreme" sport. Gradually, however, freestyle gained legitimacy as training schools emerged and rules were established to make it safer. The first World Cup freestyle events were

A group of women participate in a ski touring club in St. Moritz, Switzerland, in 1910. New types of bindings allow both downhill and cross-country skiing, depending on the terrain.

held in 1980, and freestyle skiing was a demonstration sport at the 1988 Winter Olympics. In 1992 moguls became an Olympic event, and in 1994 aerials did as well. Other forms of freestyle have since become part of World Cup and Olympic competitions.

Different Equipment

As new and different forms of skiing developed, the equipment used by skiers in each style also changed over the years. While all forms of skiing use two skis, boots, bindings, and poles, today the equipment comes in a variety of finely crafted sizes and shapes that are best suited for different purposes. The height, weight, and experience level of individual skiers also determine which types of equipment are best. With all the choices available, choosing the proper gear can be a lengthy process.

While skis originally were made of simple strips of wood, modern skis have foam or wood centers surrounded by fiberglass, steel edges, and polyethylene plastic bottoms. Most modern skis are also curved, with sidecuts (arcs) that make the center narrower than the top and bottom. These skis are known as parabolic skis. A parabola is a wide, U-shaped curve where any point inside the curve lies an equal distance from a point known as the focus. The sidecuts on a parabolic ski make the ski's edges form a parabola when the ski is flat.

Parabolic skis are also called carving skis because they allow skiers to perform a type of turn called a carving turn. In the book *Ski Skills,* ski instructor Andrzej Peszek writes that the introduction of carving skis in the 1990s was largely responsible for an immense increase in the popularity of skiing: "Beginners progress faster in them, and they enable advanced skiers to do tricks they could only dream of in the days of classical skis."[8]

An infinite variety of carved and uncarved skis exist for many purposes and combinations of purposes, such as all-mountain or Alpine touring skis for skiers who do both downhill and cross-country skiing; powder skis for skiers who ski in soft, powdery snow; racing skis for advanced Alpine skiers; jumping skis; and many other types. Skiers

SIDECUT RADIUS AND TYPES OF SKIS

The curve in the narrower part of the ski is called a sidecut. The radius of the arc of the sidecut is related to the maximum radius of a carved turn. Skis with smaller sidecut radii make smaller, tighter turns when the ski is being carved, and skis with larger sidecut radii make larger turns. The radii on skis vary to suit the skiing style.

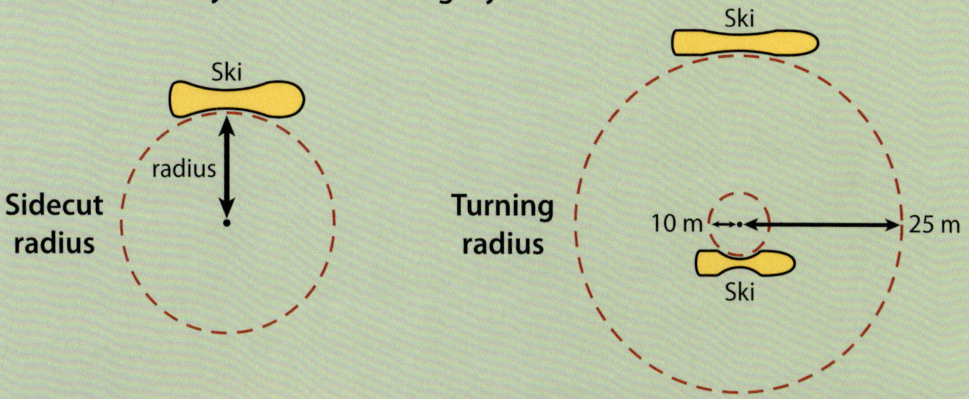

Radius (R)	Type of Ski	Description
10m–12m	Slalom	These skis will make small, aggressive turns when carved, intended for small slalom race turns.
14m–20m	Allround, Freestyle, Beginner, Powder	Most types of ski generally have radii within this range. These skis are generally a bit more stable at higher speeds than slalom skis, and are well suited to general piste skiing at the speeds that most people ski at.
20m–30m	Giant Slalom, Freestyle, Powder	Giant slalom skis make larger turns when carved and need to be used at higher speeds to work properly. They are intended for larger giant slalom turns, at speeds toward the top end of what people generally ski at on an open piste. Freestyle and powder skis can also have radii within this range, as they are not used to carve aggressively and are not intended to be skied with the same speed and aggression as giant slalom skis.
30m +	Super-G, Downhill	These skis are only really used by racers, as the speeds needed to use them properly are too fast and dangerous for most pistes.

Source: "Skis," Mechanics of Sport. www.mechanicsofsport.com/skiing/equipment/skis.html.

today can also purchase or rent a wide variety of other equipment, such as poles and boots, that are custom-made for different skiers and for different types of skiing.

The vast choices of precisely crafted equipment today have made this type of equipment expensive, but have also increased skiers' enjoyment of the sport, and this is one reason that all types of skiing continue to increase in popularity worldwide. Ski resorts, which now offer hotel accommodations, ski lessons, and mechanical lifts to make trekking up mountains easy, are also part of the attraction of skiing as a popular vacation activity for families and people of all ages. However, the main reason skiing is so popular, writes Peszek, is that "Skiing is an activity that combines fun with physical effort and skill. The fun comes mainly from the excitement of traveling at high speeds and the sense of achievement from keeping your balance on an unpredictable and uneven surface."[9]

Today there are approximately 200 million skiers worldwide, ranging from casual recreational skiers to elite competitors. In the United States, nearly 20 million people participate in snow sports, with Alpine and Nordic skiing being the most popular. Modern skiing has come a long way since the earliest skiers used simple wooden sticks to help them get places and survive snowbound winters. Although many people in cold, mountainous areas still use skiing for transportation, today the vast majority participate for recreation and competition. Whatever the reasons, the basics of skiing—two skis bound to boots, ski poles, and warmly dressed skiers moving through the snow—have not changed over the centuries.

CHAPTER 2

Snow, Skis, and Skiers: The Physics of Skiing

Skiing depends on physical interactions between a skier, his skis and other equipment, and snow. The manner in which these factors affect each other is determined by the scientific principles of physics and biomechanics. Physics is the science that defines and explains interactions between physical objects and substances. Biomechanics explains how physics affects human motion.

Frozen Water

Snow influences every aspect of a skier's technique and speed. Although most skiers do not formally analyze the properties of snow, physicists David Lind and Scott P. Sanders write in their book *The Physics of Skiing*:

> Skiers who know something about the physical nature of snow . . . will understand more about the feel of skiing: why their skis turn in one manner in the early morning but with an entirely different feel on the same slope later that day in the afternoon, and why they prefer to ski on snow that the ski report calls packed powder rather than on snow referred to as hard packed.[10]

Snow and ice are both forms of solid water. Water can exist as a liquid, steam, or solid, depending on temperature and humidity. At 212°F (100°C), water boils and turns to steam. At 32°F (0°C), it freezes into a solid state that can take any of several forms when it falls from the clouds. These forms include snow, hail (frozen rain), sleet (part water, part ice), and graupel (ice mixed with snow).

Snow falls as crystals called snowflakes, which form in cold weather when ice crystals in clouds grow around dust particles. Depending on temperature and humidity, these crystals can grow into many types of snowflakes, including stars, plates, columns, and needles. At 28.4°F (-2°C), for example, ice crystals are most likely to grow into star- or plate-shaped snowflakes. At 23°F (-5°C), needle or column shapes are most common. These differences occur because

The Sciences Behind Skiing

The sciences behind skiing encompass numerous areas of scientific inquiry.

Physics: Explains the qualities and relationships between physical objects, applies to the interactions between athletes, their equipment, and their environment.

Exercise physiology: Studies how the human body adapts and functions during physical activity.

Biomechanics: A subscience of kinesiology (the science of movement), studies how physics and mechanics apply to human movement.

Sports medicine: The area of science involved with preventing and treating sports injuries.

Sports psychology: A subdiscipline of sports medicine that deals with the mental aspects of sports.

Professionals who work in these fields are doctors of medicine, physics, kinesiology, psychology, and related fields. Several types of therapists, such as physical therapists and other rehabilitation specialists, are not doctors, but also play a huge role in sports medicine. Athletic coaches and trainers, who often have degrees in kinesiology, are also very familiar with the physical and mental aspects of sports training and competition.

temperature and humidity affect how ice crystals accumulate on dust and other matter.

Snowflakes lose their shape and become more rounded within minutes to hours after they hit the ground, because the edges melt and evaporate. The rounded crystals stick together, combining with snow that is already on the ground to create what is known as the snowpack.

The Snowpack

The snowpack actually consists of layers of snow and ice, since its top layer often melts during sunny days and freezes into ice at night. Then, more falling snow lands on top of the ice layer, creating different types of snowpacks. Physicist Mark Denny explains in *Gliding for Gold: The Physics of Winter Sports:* "Snow can be hard or soft, compacted or fluffy, with a high or low water content. All of these factors . . . influence the ease with which a ski glides over snow."[11]

Humidity in the air strongly affects snowpack quality and skiing conditions. For example, in coastal areas where evaporation from the ocean creates moisture in the air, the snowpack tends to be very tightly packed, because heavy,

Skiers in Vail, Colorado, enjoy champagne powder—a very lightweight, fluffy snow—in 2011.

Snowpack Dangers

Once snow falls to the ground, the individual snowflakes do not stick together until the snow is compacted from its own weight or from people or other forces packing it down. Until this happens, the snowpack is unstable. This instability can result in an avalanche, or torrent of rushing snow, on steep slopes with lots of new snow. Once the snowflakes bind together, the snowpack stabilizes, and the chances of an avalanche are reduced.

However, when new layers of snow fall over a period of time, the melting and refreezing as temperatures change can make the layers unstable again. Avalanches can again occur, and ski conditions may become unfavorable because very wet layers of snow are heavy and create excessive resistance to movement. In other situations where layers of snow fail to become packed down, skiers can fall through several layers and become stuck in the heavy snow. Another hazard can result from the top layer of a snowpack melting on a sunny day and refreezing into a slippery layer of ice at night.

wet snow sticks together better than snow with less moisture. Scientists say this happens because the molecules that compose water sit closest together when water is in its liquid state.

Different types of snowpacks in different areas have led skiers to describe these snowpacks with a variety of nicknames. For instance, heavy, wet snow on the Pacific coast is known as California concrete. Sierra cement refers to the drier, hard-packed snow in the inland Sierra Nevada mountains in California. Champagne powder is very lightweight, fluffy snow commonly found in Utah and Nevada. East Coast ice refers to snow with a slippery layer of ice that is difficult to ski on.

Like icy snow, a heavy, wet snowpack is also difficult to ski on. This is because skiers exert a great deal of energy plowing through heavy snow. Snow that is not tightly packed down makes skiing difficult for a similar reason—the skier and skis must press down to pack the snow tightly enough to form a stable surface. If the skier sinks into an unpacked area and has to dig out by pushing aside the snow, this can be especially energy-intensive, leaving less energy for proper technique and speed. Skiers thus prefer to ski on hard-packed dry powder since it allows them to glide freely and quickly.

Modern Alpine and Nordic ski resorts and competition sites pack and groom (smooth out) the snow to help skiers ski their best. Most of the time, only adventure skiers who venture into backcountry areas must navigate through whatever snow conditions exist in nature. Ski resorts also make and spray artificial snow to ensure ideal ski conditions when not enough natural snow falls.

Forces and Motion

> **FRESH POWDER**
>
> **Over 80**
>
> Types of snow identified by scientists. The type of snow on the ground influences the ease and speed of skiing.

Skiing on ideally packed and groomed snow is one way in which skiers control the forces that influence their energy expenditure and motion. Forces determine how objects (or living beings) move and interact. A force is simply a push or pull on an object. Scientists measure forces in units called newtons. One newton equals the amount of force needed to accelerate (speed up) something weighing one kilogram at a rate of one meter per second squared.

Forces can be internal (generated by a person's muscles) or external (generated by objects). External forces can be either contact or field forces. Contact forces exist between objects that are touching each other, such as the forces between a ski and the snow on which it glides. Field forces act at a distance. The force of gravity, which results from the earth pulling smaller objects to its center, is an example of a field force.

The main principles of physics that describe the interactions of all types of forces were formulated by British physicist Isaac Newton in the 1600s and are known as Newton's laws of motion. Newton's first law states that an object at rest will stay at rest and an object in motion will stay in motion at the same speed and direction unless an outside force acts to change the object's velocity. Velocity is not the same as speed. Speed measures how much distance something covers in a specific amount of time, while velocity measures speed and direction.

Newton's first law is sometimes called the law of inertia because it describes the principles of inertia and momentum. Inertia is the tendency of an object at rest to remain at rest. It increases with the mass of the object. In other words, more force is needed to move a more massive object from a resting position than is needed to move a less massive one. Mass is

FRESH POWDER

The friction between skis and snow is about ten times greater than that between ice and ice skates.

a measurement of how much matter an object contains. It differs from weight, since weight depends on gravity and mass does not. An object's mass is the same on earth as it is in a place such as the moon, which lacks gravity.

Momentum is the opposite of inertia. Once a force puts an object in motion, momentum keeps it moving unless another force slows or stops it. Momentum, like inertia, depends partly on an object's mass. A more massive object has more momentum than a smaller, lighter-weight object does, so more force is needed to slow or stop it. Momentum also depends on velocity. An object moving with greater velocity has greater momentum. This momentum is calculated by multiplying mass times velocity.

Newton's Other Laws

Newton's second law explains more about how the total, or net, forces affect inertia, momentum, and velocity. It states that the amount a moving object accelerates is directly proportional to the net external forces acting on the object and is inversely proportional to the object's mass. This means that applying more force to an object makes it speed up faster and that more massive objects do not accelerate as quickly as less massive ones do when the same force is applied. Physicists use the equation $f = ma$ (force equals mass times acceleration) to describe this relationship. When applied to skiing, Newton's second law means that if two skiers of different sizes push off with the same amount of force, the smaller skier will accelerate faster than the larger one.

Newton's third law further explains how forces interact. It states that every action creates an equally forceful and opposite reaction. This means that when a skier stands and exerts a force (determined by his weight) on the ground, the ground exerts an equal and opposite force on the skier. This type of force is called a ground reaction force. If the skier is standing on soft snow and the reaction force the snow

Man-Made Snow

When adequate amounts of natural snow do not fall at ski resorts, workers create artificial snow so skiers can ski. The process for making artificial snow uses some of the same mechanisms that occur naturally in clouds. First, high-pressure air guns called snow guns shoot water about 30 feet (9.14m) into the air over a ski slope. The water contains chemicals made from bacterial proteins or other substances that help water droplets quickly freeze into ice crystals known as seeded droplets before they fall to the ground.

The substances used to seed these droplets are called ice-nucleating agents. In natural clouds, dust and salt that evaporates from oceans often serve as the ice-nucleating agents that water droplets stick to as they begin to freeze into ice crystals. Chemists make some artificial ice-nucleating agents by freeze-drying certain bacteria to kill them. They then extract the proteins that the bacteria made. These proteins spur water droplets to freeze quickly. One bacterial protein often used for this purpose comes from *Pseudomonas syringae* bacteria that grow in corn plants.

Once the water droplets freeze and hit the ground, huge fans blow the artificial snow over the mountain slopes. Experts say one advantage of artificial snow is that it tends to be denser and packs more firmly than natural snow.

exerts is not equal to the force exerted by the skier's weight, he will sink into the snow until it compacts enough to push back with equal force.

Reaction forces resulting from how hard a skier presses on his skis and poles greatly influence a skier's motion and velocity in all types of skiing. In cross-country skiing, for example, "Skier generated reaction forces at the poles and skis are a competitor's primary means of moving down the ski tracks,"[12] reads an excerpt from *The Handbook of Sports Medicine and Science: Cross Country Skiing*.

WHY A SKIER SLIDES

Two primary forces are at work when a ski is on a slope: the motion force from the skier and the friction force from the snow. The motion force is created both by gravity, which is pushing the skier down on the slope, and by the movements of the skier. If the two forces are equal, the skier stops. But usually the motion force is much larger than the friction force.

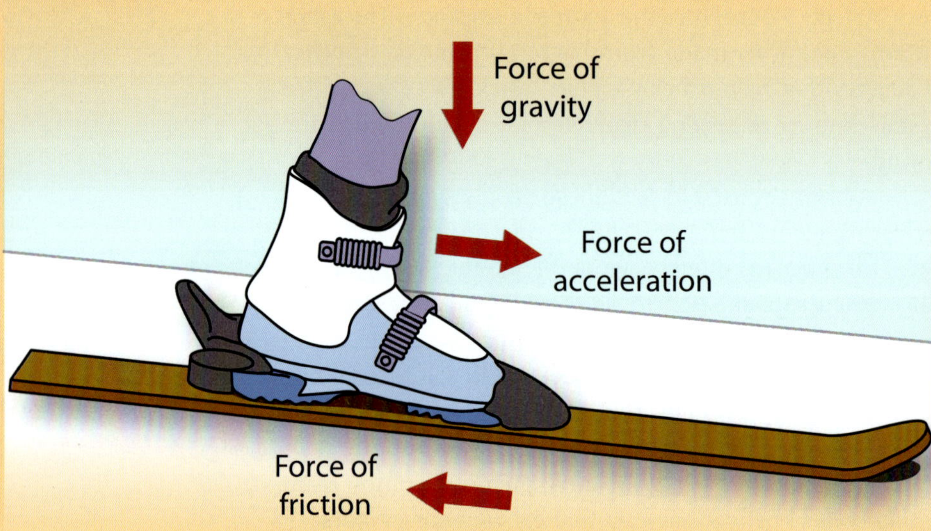

Friction Forces

In addition to reaction forces, gravity and several types of friction are the main forces involved in helping or hindering skiers' motion and speed. Frictional forces create resistance that holds a skier or other moving object back. In order for friction to occur, two objects or substances must be in contact. All objects have microscopic ridges and bumps, and friction between two objects results partly from these ridges and bumps catching on each other. Friction also occurs because of chemical and electrical bonding between the molecules that make up objects or substances such as water or air.

The types of friction that affect skiing are sliding friction, lubricated friction, and aerodynamic drag. Sliding friction (also known as contact or dry friction) occurs when two solid objects slide over each other. Each object's weight and surface qualities determine the amount of sliding friction that holds back the sliding motion. These qualities also determine the amount of external force that must be applied to overcome this friction. Objects that weigh more and have rough surfaces press more tightly against each other, thus increasing the amount of sliding friction. When smooth surfaces such as ice and skis slide past each other, the amount of friction is less, but still exists.

The measurement that describes the amount of force needed to overcome the sliding friction between two objects is called the coefficient of friction. Scientists quantify coefficients of friction for both moving and stationary objects. The coefficient of kinetic (moving) friction specifies the force needed to keep one object moving over another at a constant speed. As an example, the coefficient of kinetic friction for sliding a piece of metal over wood is about 0.40. This means that a force equivalent to 40 percent of the metal's weight is needed to keep it sliding at the same speed over a block of wood. The coefficient for sliding a block of heavier, rougher concrete over a block of wood is 0.62.

The coefficient of static friction quantifies the force needed to make a nonmoving object start moving over another object. This number is always larger than the coefficient of kinetic friction because it takes more force to overcome inertia than to maintain the velocity of a moving object. For example, the coefficient of static friction for sliding one block of glass over another is 0.94, while the coefficient of kinetic friction is 0.40.

Lubricated Friction

The second type of friction that applies to skiing, lubricated friction, occurs when two solid objects sliding past each other are separated by a thin layer of liquid. The liquid reduces the sliding friction between the objects; that is, it acts as a lubricant. Lubricated friction occurs, according to physicist Mark Denny, because "molecules of liquid are free to slide over one another—it is a defining property of liquids."[13] Since there is a thin layer of water between skis and snow under most conditions, the coefficient of kinetic friction for skis on snow ranges from 0.05 to 0.20, depending on several factors.

Unlike sliding friction, the amount of lubricated friction does not depend on an object's weight. Instead, it depends on an object's speed and area (how much space it covers), the thickness of the liquid layer, and the surrounding temperature. Lubricated friction increases as an object's speed and area increase and decreases as the thickness of the liquid layer increases—to a point. Once the thickness reaches a certain point, it adds a type of resistance called fluid drag to motion, and this holds the object back. Fluid drag can be visualized using the example of walking on a wet street versus walking in a swimming pool. Walking on a thin layer of water does not create fluid drag, and is therefore easier than

Ski jumper Martin Schmitt waxes his skis during a 1998 competition. Different types of waxes have different effects on the skis, such as preventing ice crystals from sticking to the bottom.

walking through a swimming pool, since deeper water does create drag.

The amount of lubricated friction also depends on temperature, and this quality is especially important in skiing. The sliding motion of skis on snow generates some heat because, as explained in a study by the US Army Corps of Engineers, "When two surfaces rub together, the mechanical energy loss is dissipated [released] in a number of forms, including noise and heat."[14] This heat usually melts a thin layer of snow under the skis, and the melted snow provides enough water to lubricate the two surfaces and reduce the sliding friction between them. When the sun melts snow and ice, this can also add a lubricating layer of water between skis and snow. However, studies have shown that if the outdoor temperature is below -13°F (-25°C), no snow under a skier's skis will melt, and this can slow the skier's speed because sliding friction is greater without a lubricant. For this reason, skiers often use ski wax on the bottoms of their skis to make the snow melt when the outdoor temperature is below -13°F. Ski wax also prevents ice crystals from sticking to the ski bottoms. Different types of ski wax have different effects.

Ski Waxes and Friction

Skiers can choose from many types of ski wax to decrease or increase the amount of sliding friction on their skis. The waxes used depend on the type of skis, snow conditions, temperature, and the type of skiing. Cross-country skiers, for example, often use glide wax under the skis' tips and tails and grip, or kick, wax at the skis' centers. This reduces friction when the skier is on level ground or on a small downward slope, but adds friction to help with balance while skiing uphill. The skis' camber is responsible for which type of wax touches the snow. The camber of cross-country skis prevents the center from touching the snow when the skier's weight is evenly distributed as he or she glides on level ground or downward. When the skier walks or runs uphill, his or her weight is unevenly distributed. This pushes the centers of the skis down so they touch the ground.

Aerodynamic Drag

No matter what temperature conditions exist, a third type of friction—aerodynamic drag—also acts to slow a skier down. Aerodynamic drag results from air pushing against a moving object. Isaac Newton was among the first to recognize that the amount of aerodynamic drag depends on

Ferran Terra trains for the 2014 Winter Olympics in Russia. Tight clothing and a crouched position reduce aerodynamic drag on a skier.

the speed of the projectile (object traveling through air). As the speed of the projectile increases, the amount of aerodynamic drag increases as the squared value of the speed. For instance, if a skier's speed doubles, the amount of drag around the skier increases by a factor of four.

Drag forces also increase as air density increases. That is, the thicker air that exists at lower altitudes exerts slightly more drag than the thinner air at higher altitudes. The difference in air density at high and low altitudes can affect a skier's speed or the distance jumped by a ski jumper, and elite skiers learn to compensate for these differences by altering the angles at which they hold their body.

The size and shape of the projectile affect drag a great deal more than air density does, so skiers go to great lengths to control their overall size and the area of the body impacted by the air. The larger the size of the projectile, the greater the amount of drag. Skiers therefore wear tight-fitting clothing and crouch forward when possible to reduce the area of the body that moves directly into the air and wind. They also wear helmets designed to reduce drag. A 2010 study reported in the journal *Procedia Engineering* found that skiers who do not wear skintight clothing increase the amount of aerodynamic drag by about 5.2 percent. Other studies indicate that changing the body position from upright to tucked reduces aerodynamic drag by more than 50 percent.

An article in *The Handbook of Sports Medicine and Science: Cross Country Skiing* explains how these measures affect aerodynamic drag:

> With motion, air flows around the body, skis and poles and exerts varying pressure patterns on the front, back and sides of a skier. Streamlining of the body and equipment can smooth the air flow patterns and minimize pressure differences from front to back of a skier. . . . If a skier can reduce . . . the area upon which the pressure difference acts, . . . drag force can be reduced.[15]

The Sum of Forces

Aerodynamic drag and other types of friction act in the direction opposite a skier's movement, and the main force acting to oppose friction—particularly in downhill skiing—is gravity. Gravity is affected by the steepness of a slope, since the force of gravity always acts in a downward direction. When a skier stands on an inclined slope, the ground reaction force acting on him is at an angle to the force of gravity and cannot balance the gravity force. Mathematical calculations show that because of this imbalance, objects accelerate faster down an inclined surface than they do on a flat surface.

Other forces such as wind can act to either support or oppose gravity and friction, depending on their direction. A tailwind that pushes a skier forward opposes friction and supports gravity, and a headwind does the opposite. When a skier turns, still other forces come into play. Centripetal force is the force that pulls a rotating body toward the center of the curve that a turn follows. Centrifugal force does the opposite. Internal forces generated by the skier also contribute to the total forces that affect a skier's motion.

The sum of all of these forces at a given moment determines a skier's speed, direction, and rate of acceleration. While a skier cannot control all these forces, using the right

Didier Defago wins the gold medal at the 2010 Winter Olympics by 0.07 seconds. Because small differences in time can have a big effect on the outcome of a race, reducing friction and drag as much as possible is very important to skiers.

equipment and technique can make enough of a difference to influence winning or not winning a competition. Among elite skiers, the fractions of a second gained by diligently trying to defeat friction can be critical. For example, in the men's downhill race at the 2010 Olympics, the gold medalist, Didier Defago of Switzerland, was 0.07 seconds faster than silver medalist Aksel Lund Svindal of Norway and 0.09 seconds faster than bronze medalist Bode Miller of the United States. This is why competitive skiers spend a great deal of time choosing the right equipment and training to develop the skills they need to ski well.

CHAPTER 3

Training a Skier's Body

Skiing well requires skiers to control the interactions of forces between themselves and their environment. Achieving this control takes a great deal of practice regarding specific skills as well as training the body with exercises that promote the power, balance, strength, flexibility, agility, and endurance a good skier needs. As the book *Total Skiing* states, skiing poses a variety of physical challenges: "Imagine skiing for two to five hours over varied terrain and conditions, making short, quick turns down steep terrain and long, wide turns through flat terrain, jumping over obstacles, and bending and flexing your joints as you absorb bumpy terrain."[16] The movements involved in meeting these challenges require strong, well-conditioned muscles and cardiovascular strength. As the main body systems involved in athletic performance, the musculoskeletal and cardiovascular systems interact to allow skiers to move optimally without becoming overly fatigued.

The Cardiovascular System

The cardiovascular system, which consists of the heart, lungs, and blood vessels, is especially important for endurance (the ability to continue an activity without becoming overly tired), but it also plays a big role in supporting

Adventure skiers, such as these in the French Alps, require the most endurance and need to be in excellent aerobic condition.

the musculoskeletal system (muscles and bones). Cross-country and adventure skiing require the most endurance, but athletes who participate in other types of skiing that rely on short bursts of energy need good endurance as well. For example, a 2011 study reported in the *Journal of Sports Science and Medicine* found that downhill skiing "may be classified as an intermittent activity that requires both aerobic and anaerobic demands."[17] Aerobic (meaning "with oxygen") fitness contributes to endurance, while anaerobic (meaning "without oxygen") fitness is primarily associated with strength.

Aerobic fitness depends on how well the cardiovascular system delivers oxygen to muscles throughout the body. Oxygen enters the body through the mouth and nose and goes through the bronchial (breathing) tubes into millions of tiny sacs in the lungs called alveoli. Alveoli are surrounded by small blood vessels known as capillaries. Oxygen travels through the alveoli walls into the blood in these capillaries and latches onto a protein in red blood cells called hemoglobin. Hemoglobin carries the oxygen as the blood flows from the lungs to the heart, and then takes oxygen into cells throughout the body as the heart pumps blood via larger vessels called arteries. Cells use oxygen to produce energy, and this process produces a waste gas called carbon dioxide. Carbon dioxide is returned to the heart in blood-filled veins, and the heart sends this blood to the lungs, where alveoli take up carbon dioxide to be exhaled through the breathing tubes.

FRESH POWDER

500

Calories burned by Alpine skiing per hour. Cross-country skiing burns about 900.

Increasing Cardiovascular Fitness

Exercise increases the muscles' need for oxygen, and this affects oxygen processing by the cardiovascular system. The book *World of Sports Science* explains: "When the body is subjected to exercise, and its increased physical demands, the cardiovascular system is forced to work more quickly and more efficiently to fulfill bodily needs."[18] To accommodate these needs, the heart beats faster to pump more blood to the muscles and the lungs increase the breathing rate to take in more oxygen and let out more carbon dioxide.

With regular aerobic exercises such as running, swimming, and brisk walking, the heart muscle grows stronger and becomes more efficient at pumping blood, so it does not have to work as hard when an athlete is resting or exercising. Regular aerobic exercise also makes the alveoli in the lungs more efficient at taking in and processing oxygen. These changes in the heart and lungs can be measured as evidence of cardiovascular fitness.

One commonly used measurement of cardiovascular fitness is the VO_2 max. This test measures how much oxygen an individual is capable of using during intense exercise. The more oxygen a person can use, the better his or her endurance is. The VO_2 max depends on genetics, age, gender, and amount of body fat, in addition to being influenced by fitness training and by the type of aerobic exercises an athlete practices. Elite distance runners and

As part of his training for the 2014 Winter Olympics, skier Mohammad Karim does aerobic exercises in Islamabad, Pakistan.

swimmers, professional soccer players, and cross-country skiers tend to have the highest scores (80 to 95 milliliters of oxygen per kilogram of body weight per minute, compared to 35 to 45 ml/kg/min for the average person). In fact, according to the *Winter Sports Medicine Handbook,* "VO_2 max values . . . in elite cross-country skiers are among the highest recorded."[19]

Another factor that influences cardiovascular fitness for skiers is altitude—how high up the skiing takes place. As altitude rises, the air becomes thinner, or less dense. Air density is reduced by about 3 percent for every 1,000 feet (305m) of altitude. Because there is less oxygen to breathe at high altitudes, people who live and train at low altitudes have difficulty breathing when they ski higher up. They also become tired faster at higher altitudes because less oxygen gets to their muscles, including the heart muscle. This is why many competitive skiers train and live at high altitudes. Over time, their bodies get used to functioning with less oxygen, and their athletic performance does not suffer.

Muscles and Fitness

Good cardiovascular fitness is only part of what skiers need to master the necessary ski skills. They also need strong, flexible muscles, so a skier's training and conditioning regimen should include muscle-enhancing exercises as well as aerobic enhancement.

Humans have three main types of muscles: cardiac, smooth, and skeletal. The heart consists mostly of the cardiac muscle, which allows it to beat and pump blood. Like the smooth muscle that exists in most internal organs, the

What Affects VO_2 Max?

VO_2 max tests measure the maximum amount of oxygen a person is capable of taking in and converting to muscle energy. VO_2 max levels depend on some controllable and some uncontrollable factors.

Controllable factors:

- Individuals who do regular aerobic exercise usually have much higher VO_2 max levels than those who do not.
- Those with more muscle mass and less body fat have higher VO_2 max levels because muscle cells consume more oxygen than fat cells do.

Uncontrollable factors:

- Age—VO_2 max levels peak around age twenty and decline about 1 percent a year after age twenty-five. However, the rate of decline is slower in individuals who continue to exercise.
- Gender—Women's VO_2 max levels are about 20 percent lower than men's. Exercise physiologists believe this is mostly because women have less muscle mass and tend to store more fat than men do.
- Genetics—Differences in individuals' genes determine how well the circulatory system carries and delivers oxygen to muscles and how well muscles use oxygen. Some genes affect how well hemoglobin molecules in blood bind to and carry oxygen throughout the body. Others determine the ability of cell mitochondria to convert oxygen into ATP (adenosine triphosphate) energy. Still others affect how many ST (slow twitch) and FT (fast twitch) muscle fibers people are born with. ST fibers consume more oxygen than FT fibers do, so those with more ST fibers tend to have higher VO_2 max levels.

Higher and Higher

Exercise physiologists recommend that athletes training to compete at a specific altitude spend a few weeks living at that altitude before competing. This allows the body to acclimatize, or get used to being there. Since air pressure is lower the higher up a person goes, less oxygen is forced from alveoli in the lungs to the bloodstream. This makes breathing difficult. While adjusting to having less oxygen available at higher altitudes, an individual's heart rate and breathing rate initially increase, then gradually decrease as alveoli become more efficient. Acclimatization also involves changes in the red blood cells that carry oxygen throughout the body. The bone marrow starts producing extra red blood cells within a few days of living at higher altitudes, and these cells grow larger than normal. The amount of oxygen-carrying hemoglobin in the red blood cells also increases. These changes allow more oxygen to be transported. After several weeks, changes in muscles also occur. More capillaries grow to supply muscles with oxygen, and more mitochondria form within muscle cells to supply more power. Muscle cells also produce more myoglobin, a protein that binds to oxygen. These changes allow muscles to work more efficiently at higher altitude.

cardiac muscle works involuntarily, without an individual's conscious control. On the other hand, skeletal muscles, which are attached to bones to allow the body to move, are under voluntary control.

All muscles are composed of elastic muscle fiber cells, also known as muscle fibers. According to a Harvard Health Publications report, "One muscle may have anywhere from 10,000 to more than a million muscle fibers."[20] The parts of muscle fibers that allow muscles to stretch and contract (shorten) are proteins called actin and myosin. When these proteins slide past each other, the muscle extends or contracts to move various body parts.

There are two main types of muscle fibers: fast twitch (FT) and slow twitch (ST). ST fibers contract slowly and tire less quickly than FT fibers do, so they are most useful in movements that require endurance. FT fibers are most important in activities that involve short bursts of anaerobic energy, such as sprinting. Both types of fibers operate in response to electrical and chemical signals from neurons (nerve cells) in the brain and spinal cord. Neurons in the brain send instructions to motor neurons in the spinal cord, and each spinal motor neuron controls specific groups of muscle fibers. The neurons that control FT fibers fire off signals ten times faster than the neurons controlling ST fibers. This is why FT fibers contract and lengthen faster than ST fibers.

FRESH POWDER

People born at high altitudes develop extra lung alveoli and small blood vessels to help them breathe more easily.

Muscular Force

Motor neurons, along with the size and number of muscle fibers, also control the amount of force a muscle exerts. The more muscle fibers a motor neuron controls and the faster the neuron communicates with these fibers, the more force the entire muscle generates. FT fibers generate more force than ST fibers, so athletes who need stronger muscles seek to enlarge FT fibers with strength-training exercises. A Harvard Health Publications article explains that strength-training exercises also act on motor neurons: "Strength training enhances the ability of the nervous system to activate motor units [groups of muscle fibers]."[21] Athletes who need endurance, on the other hand, seek to enlarge ST fibers through training with aerobic activities.

The force a muscle exerts also depends on its overall size; bigger muscles generate more force. Since strength-training exercises enlarge muscles as well as muscle fibers, many athletes use these exercises to build muscle mass. One effective method of achieving this goal utilizes weights or other types of resistance such as elastic bands. Exercising against resistance overworks muscles, leading to small tears that the body

Swedish skier Anja Paerson exercises at the gym in the Olympic Village in Whistler, British Columbia, in 2010.

repairs in several days. The repair process enlarges muscles because damaged muscle fibers release chemicals called growth factors, which cause satellite cells outside the muscle fibers to reproduce and fuse with the fibers. This process then causes muscle fibers to produce more of the proteins actin and myosin. The additional satellite cells and proteins enlarge the muscle, and having more actin and myosin pulling and pushing the muscle fibers increases the muscle's strength.

Muscle size and strength can also be enhanced through anaerobic exercises such as short sprints. Here, muscle cells break down sugars for energy through a process called glycolysis. Glycolysis produces a by-product called lactic acid, which triggers biochemical events that enlarge muscles. Lactic acid also leads to muscle soreness, so athletes must be careful not to overdo these exercises.

Muscle Fuel

Glycolysis is only one of three methods by which muscles generate the fuel they need to operate. Muscle cells use a substance called ATP (adenosine triphosphate) as fuel, and

HOW STRENGTH TRAINING BUILDS MUSCLE MASS

Weight lifting, resistance training, and other exercises create microscopic tears in the muscle fibers. To fix a tear, satellite cells outside the muscle fiber are activated. The satellite cells fuse together and with the muscle fiber, so each repair adds more cells to the muscle fiber, making it larger and stronger.

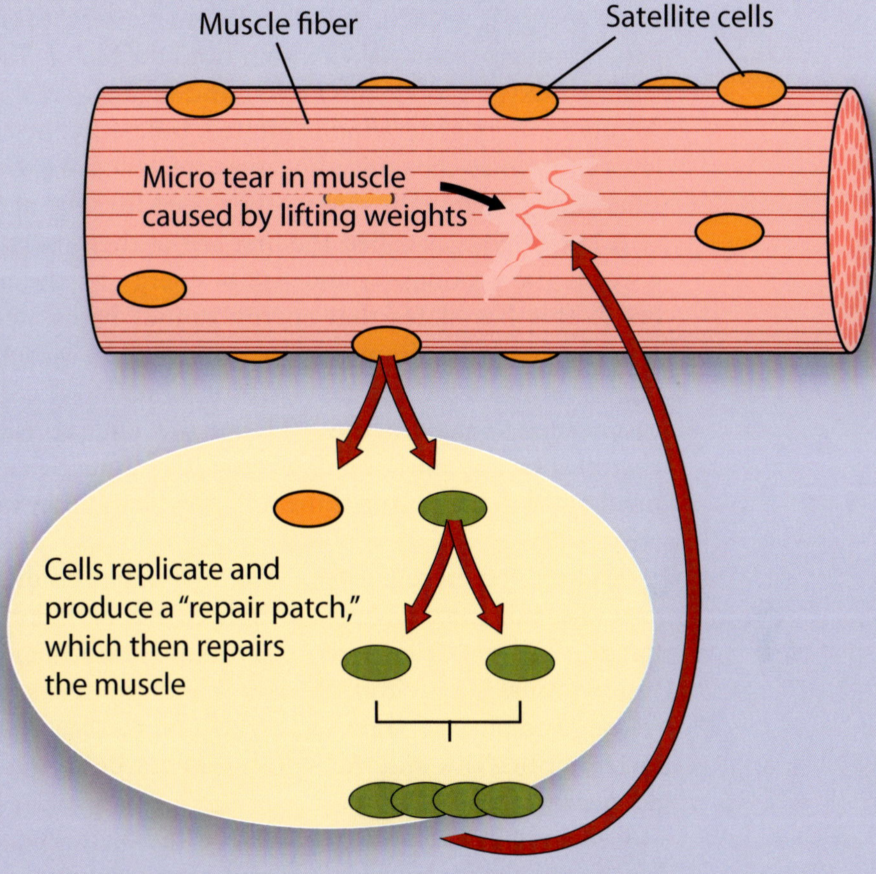

they produce ATP by transforming other cellular chemicals. These energy-generating processes occur in the part of the cell called the mitochondria.

In the first process, muscle cells convert phosphocreatine into ATP. Phosphocreatine is a chemical that muscle cells make from proteins they obtain from food. Most phosphocreatine in the human body is stored in muscle cells. The process in which muscle cells convert phosphocreatine into ATP is anaerobic and can only be sustained for about ten seconds. When muscles need more energy, cells use the anaerobic process of glycolysis to produce ATP from glucose in cells or from glycogen (sugar stored in the liver). This chemical reaction can be sustained for about two minutes. If more energy is needed, muscle cells use the aerobic energy-generating process to take oxygen from the blood. The cells then use oxygen to burn both fats and sugars to make ATP. Aerobic energy generation is limited, time-wise, by an athlete's endurance capability. For instance, elite cross-country skiers can generate the energy they need for several hours.

A law of physics called the first law of thermodynamics governs the production and use of energy by the human body. This law states that energy cannot be created, but must be converted from one form to another. Muscle cells convert nutrients they receive from food into the chemicals needed to manufacture ATP, and they then convert this chemical energy into kinetic energy. Thus, muscle cells depend on food to give them the building blocks they need to create energy.

Athletes therefore need to eat a well-balanced diet consisting of adequate protein, carbohydrates, and fats to obtain the nutrients they need for optimum performance. The International Ski Federation Medical Committee notes that "Skiing and physical training can be both an aerobic and an anaerobic activity, and the fuel sources for both need to be adequately replaced."[22]

Cells obtain the glycogen used as the primary anaerobic energy source from simple and complex carbohydrates such as sugars, fruits, vegetables, cereals, bread, and pasta. Dieticians recommend that athletes ingest mostly complex carbohydrates like pasta, rice, vegetables, and whole grains rather than simple carbohydrates such as candy, cake, and other sweets because complex carbohydrates raise blood sugar slowly and provide longer-lasting energy. Athletes also need an adequate fat intake because muscle cells burn some fats for energy, and they need enough proteins such as meat, poultry, and dairy products to help build muscles and repair muscle damage.

Skiers also need the vitamins and minerals that come from nutritious foods to help repair the muscle damage that comes from strenuous exercise. A 2010 study in Spain found that adventure skiers who ingest the most nutritious diets show the least muscle damage after a two-day race. The researchers recommend that ideally, "skiers should have high intakes of total energy, macronutrients [proteins, fats, and carbohydrates], vitamins A and B, Na [sodium], Zn [zinc], and Fe [iron] in order to decrease the deleterious effect of strenuous exercise."[23] Since adventure skiers expend such large amounts of energy, they also have to ingest far more calories than most people do in order to keep up with their energy and cell repair demands. According to the study, the average male adventure skier needs at least 4,400 calories per day to avoid severe muscle damage and fatigue. Most nonathlete adult males take in 2,500 to 3,000 calories per day.

Energy Gel

A study reported in the *Journal of Sports Science and Medicine* in 2012 explored the question of whether a nutritional supplement helps athletic performance. Researchers tested a carbohydrate-protein energy gel on competitive slalom skiers to see if it improved their success in finishing races. They hypothesized that ingesting a concentrated gel would be more helpful than ingesting large amounts of liquid protein and carbohydrate supplements right before a race, and the study proved this hypothesis was correct. When compared to liquid supplements and to a placebo (a fake substance that looks like the real thing), the gel significantly improved racing performance and led to less-fatigued skiers.

The researchers believe the improvements occurred because the gel increases levels of the chemicals myoglobin and creatine kinase in the body. Both are important in muscle activity and energy production. They believe the gel may also diminish levels of brain chemicals that promote fatigue. This may help the brain continue to activate muscle fibers longer.

Training Exercises

Providing muscles with the nutritional building blocks they need for generating energy is only part of the total training program skiers need in order to perform their best. Since skiing well requires both aerobic and anaerobic fitness, training programs incorporate exercises that promote endurance and strength, along with the other qualities of balance, power, flexibility, and agility that skiers require.

Emily Cook, a member of the U.S. aerial ski team, does push-ups on medicine balls as part of a fitness program that will develop agility and strength.

Balance is especially important for skiing. Indeed, skiing is often referred to as "balance in motion." Ski coach Andrzej Peszek writes in *Ski Skills,* "skiing involves a continuous rebalancing of our center of gravity on skis that are moving over terrain that's constantly changing in both direction and texture. It's hard to imagine a tougher challenge to our sense of balance."[24] Good balance, in turn, requires stability and mobility. Stability is the ability to stay upright when outside forces act to change one's position. Mobility (also known as agility) allows the body to move in all directions while coordinating and controlling these movements. Muscles, along with bones, joints, tendons (cartilage that connects muscles to bones), ligaments (cartilage that connects bones to each other), and the balance organs in the inner ears work together to control balance, stability, and mobility.

Exercises that enhance these qualities train an athlete to stay upright and balanced while at rest and in motion. One commonly used ski training exercise involves squatting or lunging on one or two feet while standing on disks called stability disks. Squats and lunges on one foot that are performed on flat ground also help with balance. In another balance-enhancing exercise, two people stand facing each other with their knees and hips flexed and their arms held out straight in front of the chest. The individuals push forward with their hands until the two sets of hands touch, and both people try to knock the other off balance. With practice, both learn to stay upright.

Flexibility, Strength, and Power

Exercises that improve flexibility, strength, and power can also help a skier develop good balance, stability, and mobility. Flexibility, or the ability to stretch the muscles without pain, can be improved with stretching exercises such as bending over and touching the ground with the hands. Other flexibility exercises that skiers commonly perform improve hip flexibility, which is important because skiers must learn to turn their legs without turning their upper bodies when they execute turns in the snow. In one such exercise, an athlete lies on his back on the floor and extends his legs straight out in front while extending his arms out to the side. He then raises his legs into an "L" position. Keeping his back flat against the floor, he then lowers his legs to the floor on one side of the body and holds the position for about ten seconds. Then he lowers his legs to the other side and repeats the pattern several times.

Strength and power are also critical for skiers. According to the National Strength and Conditioning Association's *Performance Training Journal*, "Strength is the ability to produce or generate force. . . . Power is the ability to produce or generate force quickly."[25] Thus, an athlete who can perform five squats in four seconds is generating more power than one who does five squats in ten seconds, even though their strength may be identical.

A popular type of power-enhancing exercise is plyometrics. This involves stretching a muscle group before contracting it. One common plyometric exercise is doing a squat to pre-stretch the leg muscles before jumping up. The squat stores energy in the muscles being stretched and therefore adds power to make the jump faster and higher than it would have been without the squat. When done repeatedly, plyometric exercises make the muscles routinely contract faster and more forcefully.

Strength-training exercises are not performed as quickly as power-training exercises are. In addition, as ski coach Chris Fellows writes in his book *Total Skiing,* strength-training exercises for skiing differ from those for many other sports because "skiing requires a different type of strength. Muscle strength for skiing is about balance, powerful movements in a wide range of motion, increased joint stability, and muscle coordination."[26] Thus, strength-training exercises for skiers incorporate measures to improve balance as the muscles are strengthened. Rather than just lifting weights, for example, a skier will lift weights while doing lunges or squats or will do push-ups on a balance ball. These types of exercises strengthen muscles throughout the body, which is especially important since skiing requires strong arms, legs, hips, abdomen, and other body parts.

Ski Skills Training

In addition to doing exercises in a gym or outdoors in a non-ski setting, skiers perform skills drills on snow-covered slopes of varying steepness. In a lateral step drill, for instance, skiers stand on a slope and push off with their ski poles. They then alternate stepping sideways to the left and right to practice shifting their weight from ski to ski. In another drill, skiers hop and land on snow while learning how to bend their ankles, knees, and hips to absorb the landing forces and to stay balanced. Other drills teach skiers how to properly angle the upper and lower body on slopes of different steepness. Mastering these angles helps with balance, since holding the body at the proper angle distributes the person's weight evenly and balances it over the skis.

Depending on the type of skiing a skier chooses, other skills drills help with learning and perfecting the specific movements involved. Good skiers practice the necessary skills over and over and maintain excellent physical fitness so they can perform and compete optimally. Experts find that most of the time skiers who put the most time and effort into their fitness and skills training are the most successful competitors. As an example, the authors of a 2012 study on slalom racing write that the "quantity and quality of training often dictates racing success."[27] However, physical training is not the only important element in skiing and competing well. The mental aspects of skiing play an equally important role.

CHAPTER 4

Courage and Other Mental Powers: Psychology and Skiing

As important as physical training and skills are for skiing performance, the mental aspects are equally critical for both recreational and competitive skiers. In an article in *Ski Racing*, sports psychologist Jim Taylor states, "Whenever I talk to racers and coaches, I ask them what aspect of ski racing seems to have the greatest impact on how they perform. Almost unanimously they say the mental part."[28]

The area of psychology that deals with the mental and emotional components of sports is called sports psychology. Sports psychologists help athletes deal with issues such as thinking, motivation, focus, confidence, courage, and decision-making. Ski coaches and trainers also do much to enhance athletes' mental and emotional strength through positive teaching techniques and attention to each person's state of mind.

The Power of Motivation

One of the most important factors in determining a skier's success in learning and perfecting skills and in winning competitions is motivation—the drive to work hard to achieve a goal. Regardless of a skier's inborn ability, those who are motivated to do well are willing to put in the time and effort to do whatever it takes to improve. Using ski racing as an example, Jim Taylor writes:

> Motivation in ski racing is so important because you must be willing to work hard in the face of fatigue, boredom, pain, and the desire to do other things. Motivation will impact everything that influences your ski racing: physical conditioning, technical and tactical training, equipment, preparation, mental readiness, and general lifestyle including sleep, diet, school or work, and relationships.[29]

Motivation can be intrinsic or extrinsic. Intrinsic motivation comes from the desire to learn a skill, improve one's performance, and excel at a sport because the individual truly enjoys the sport and the feeling of accomplishment that accompanies performing well. Extrinsic motivation involves the desire to win external measures of success, such as medals, prestige, or money. Extrinsic motivation can also be driven by a desire to impress or not let down a coach, team, or other individual. Sports psychologists believe that athletes who possess both intrinsic and extrinsic motivation make the best competitors. Those who are driven only by extrinsic motivation tend to become discouraged when they fail to meet others' expectations, and those who rely only on intrinsic motivation often lack the competitive spirit to excel in competition. Competitive success is most likely when athletes derive satisfaction both from doing well and from receiving recognition for their achievements. For recreational skiers, having intrinsic motivation is sufficient.

Chad Giese participates in a 2001 cross-country event. For him, skiing is about more than just winning competitions.

Disability, Mental Health, and Skiing

Skiing is not only an exciting sport for able-bodied individuals. Many disabled people also benefit physically and psychologically. One of the best-known programs that make it possible for disabled individuals to ski is the Miracles on a Mountainside clinic in Colorado. Recreation therapist Santo Trombetta started the clinic (originally called the National Disabled Veterans Winter Sports Clinic) in the 1980s to help keep a disabled soldier active during the winter months. Trombetta strapped the man, who was a paraplegic, into a special bucket seat on skis. Despite numerous setbacks, the veteran was so exhilarated by the experience that he continued to ski. Trombetta's clinic has made similar experiences available to many other disabled veterans, and today it hosts the largest disabled winter sports events in the world.

Trombetta states in a *Paraplegia News* article, "It changes people forever. It's about overcoming challenges, healing, and living life to the fullest. It's that moment when a disabled veteran suddenly stops focusing on what he or she can't do and realizes a whole new world of possibilities."

Air Force veteran Sheila Iames, who suffered a spinal cord injury in 2009, is one veteran who found skiing to be emotionally liberating. She said, "I feel like I am floating! Right now I feel like a big balloon. This is so awesome! I can't believe I actually did it!" Before her injury, Iames was afraid to ski.

Quoted in Elaine Buehler. "The jewel in the crown: for 25 years, 'miracles' have taken place on a mountainside in Colorado, where veterans with disabilities can find a whole new world of possibilities." *Paraplegia News*, June 2011, p. 22.

Both types of motivation contain different elements with different degrees of importance for different people. For some athletes, the desire to compete in the Olympics may be the primary motivating factor. For others, such as elite

Skiers participate in the 2008 Miracles on a Mountainside clinic, an event held annually in Colorado that helps disabled people experience skiing.

cross-country skier Chad Giese, different factors drive a devotion to the sport. Giese writes:

> What motivates me to train hard and compete is most likely the same thing that motivates you to train and compete. Being a cross-country skier opens up the best of what life has to offer. I get out of bed on 40°F rainy days in October because I like the fresh smell of the rain. I go into the woods for 6 hour runs because I love looking at the leaves, the rocks, the animals, the beautiful views, the sky, the sun and countless other reasons. . . . Great results [winning races] are a nice reward for all of the hard work I put in throughout the year, but they are not the main reason I ski.[30]

Focusing on Goals

Whatever a skier's motivation may be, it must be translated into goal-setting and mental focus to lead an athlete to success. Goals can be immediate, short-term, or long-term, and sports psychologists say that setting concrete, well-defined goals of all types is most likely to lead to success in meeting these goals. For example, if a skier sets the goal of improving

FRESH POWDER

Different goals motivate different skiers. Examples of these goals are having fun, feeling a thrill, mastering a skill, and breaking a world record.

his or her downhill racing time by five seconds within three months, the skier can then focus on improving specific skills to reach this goal.

Most of the goal-directed focusing skills that ski coaches and sports psychologists emphasize involve concentrating on a series of immediate concerns without being distracted by other thoughts. During training, coaches teach skiers to concentrate on one aspect of a skill at a time. For instance, one focus point might be paying attention to the position of one's feet while learning to turn on skis. Once this part of the skill is mastered, the focus can shift to another element, such as turning the legs without turning the upper body.

During competitions, coaches emphasize a tight focus on immediate concerns as well. Julie Sloan, a ski coach with a degree in sports psychology, coaches a successful high school ski team and believes her emphasis on focusing on one thing at a time is responsible for giving her team a competitive edge. "Don't focus on the finish line; focus on the first gate," she tells her slalom skiers. "Control the controllable. At the start of a race you can only control what's in front of you, and that's the first gate."[31]

In other situations, coaches and psychologists emphasize focusing on other relevant things or events. For example, sports psychologist Barbara Meyer teaches her clients to focus on how their muscles and other body parts feel when they are performing well. Meyer then encourages athletes to focus on replicating those feelings every time they practice or compete.

Decision-Making and Confidence

When applied to training and competitive situations, the ability to focus helps skiers make good decisions in a constantly changing environment. With changes in terrain, ranging from bumps and hills to trees, skiers must quickly decide how far forward their body must lean, how far apart

Experience and Decision-Making

Skiers often make smart decisions based on past experience. However, sometimes people who are usually careful let their guard down with disastrous results. One widely known example that occurred in 1995 cost experienced adventure skier Steve Carruthers his life. Carruthers and two friends decided to ski in an area in Utah known for its avalanches, thinking it looked safe. According to an Association for Psychological Science article, "More than a hundred metric tons of snow roared down the mountainside at fifty miles an hour, blanketing the slope and pinning Carruthers against an aspen." Carruthers' friends survived, but all three were widely criticized for taking a foolish risk despite their vast experience.

A close friend of Carruthers named Ian McCammon wanted to know what led athletes like Carruthers to make faulty decisions, so he published a study that analyzed hundreds of avalanche-related deaths. McCammon found that "heuristic traps" were usually responsible for these faulty decisions. Heuristics are mental shortcuts people use to make everyday decisions. Without heuristics, every little decision would require careful thought.

Psychologists have identified many types of heuristics. One type is the "familiar experience" heuristic. Usually, this heuristic saves time, as in instances where a shopper chooses a familiar brand of soap because it worked well in the past. But in Carruthers' case, the skiers "were so familiar with the terrain that it seemed safe—simply because it had always been safe before." McCammon found that several other heuristics, such as the "acceptance" heuristic, also came into play for Carruthers. This heuristic makes people more likely to do risky things when they are with a group and want to fit in.

"Heuristics Revealed." Association for Psychological Science, October 2010. www.psychologicalscience.org/index.php/publications/observer/2010/october-10/heuristics-revealed.html.

Sports PTSD

Sports psychologist Alan Goldberg calls one emotional disorder that athletes often deal with Sports PTSD. PTSD (post-traumatic stress disorder) can occur in people who experience frightening events such as being attacked or fighting in a war. The individual has terrifying flashbacks that impair his or her ability to sleep and function. In Sports PTSD, the triggering event is suffering or witnessing a serious injury. The resulting mental trauma can affect athletic performance immediately or sometimes long after the experience. Goldberg describes the effects on skiing as, "The trauma is alive and well within the athlete stealing her heart and courage, feeding her tentativeness and making a smooth, fluid execution impossible."

PTSD results from brain cells continuing to trigger the production of high levels of anxiety and stress-related chemicals such as norepinephrine and cortisol. Goldberg and others tried treating Sports PTSD-related performance problems with typical psychological and behavioral therapies for many years, but found these therapies ineffective. However, he and other therapists have found that EMDR (eye movement desensitization and reprocessing) therapy can help. In EMDR, patients move their eyes back and forth in patterns that stimulate both sides of the brain, while focusing on the fears associated with the traumatic event. This has been proven to "rebalance" nerve cell firing in the brain and also helps restore the production of anxiety-related chemicals to normal levels.

Alan Goldberg. "So What Kind of a Head Do You Have on Your Shoulders?" Competitive Advantage. www.competitivedge.com/catalog/skiing.

their skis should move, how sharp a turn must be, and other details that affect how they go about avoiding obstacles in their path. These split-second decisions, which are based on experience, can make the difference between winning or losing a race and between staying safe or tumbling down a mountain. For competitive skiers, these split-second decisions also affect the overall racing strategy. For example, if skiers choose to take a slower, wider turn, they may have to make up for lost fractions of a second by speeding up another turn.

Much of a skier's ability to consistently make smart, fast, tactical decisions comes from self-confidence as well as experience. Without confidence, a skier may hesitate and lose valuable time evaluating a situation rather than relying on first impressions. Sports psychologists find that the necessary confidence comes from hours and hours of practice that verify the wisdom of a particular decision. After much practice, the decisions become relatively automatic, so they do not require much conscious thought.

Another important element in building an athlete's confidence is competitive success. As an example, when seventeen-year-old ski champion Jill Kinmont began winning medals in national competitions in the 1950s, she asked her coach, Dave McCoy, how she could improve enough to qualify for the Olympics. McCoy told her she had flawless technique and a strong desire to win, but needed more self-confidence. "You've got everything but confidence," he said. "There's nothing [that is] going to improve your skiing outside of some more victories."[32]

Many sports psychologists say an athlete's self-confidence can be improved through cognitive therapy as well. In this form of psychotherapy, people learn to replace negative thoughts with positive ones that affirm their abilities and competence. In a slight variation on this type of therapy, sports psychologist Haley Perlus advises athletes to keep a "confidence book" where they write down specific things they do well during training. The athletes then read the book right before a competition to "prove" to themselves that they have the skills to do well.

Another confidence-building technique many psychologists recommend is visualization, or imagery. Here, an athlete imagines how a skill looks before physically performing it. Studies have shown that visualization speeds up and enhances skill learning and performance more than simply practicing the skill itself. Visualization also builds

Photo on next page: Kamil Stoch participates in a hill ski jumping training session at the 2014 Winter Olympics. The fear that some skiers may feel before an event can be helpful because the body releases certain chemicals and hormones that provide a burst of energy.

confidence in one's ability to perform the skill. For champion ski racer Steven Nyman, who suffered a serious injury in 2011, imagery was key in helping him regain the confidence to ski with his former drive and competitive spirit. Nyman worked with a psychologist to imagine every detail of a ski course: "You see [in your mind] where the turns are, where the terrain is, and you see yourself going over that terrain. You visualize this over and over and over to convince yourself of what's possible," he told *Wired* magazine.[33]

Olympic champion Lindsey Vonn also uses imagery before a race and considers this mental activity to be as important as her physical training. Vonn states in an interview, "I always visualize the run before I do it. By the time I get to the start gate, I've run that race 100 times already in my head, picturing how I'll take the turns."[34]

Fear and Skiing

Visualization and building self-confidence in general are also effective in helping skiers overcome fear, which is one of the most significant barriers to success in skiing. Much has been written about the role of fear in skiing because it is considered to be a risky sport and because many competitive skiers are known to be daredevils. Sports psychologists say that while fear is a natural response to the prospect of speeding down a steep mountainside or jumping off a cliff, too much fear can impair performance by making the body stiff and unable to move in the fluid, agile manner that skiing demands. Fear can also interfere with skiers' focus on their surroundings, and an excessive amount of fear can prevent some people from skiing at all. At the same time, too little fear can lead skiers to take dangerous risks that result in severe injuries.

Sports psychologist Haley Perlus writes in an article in *Podium Sports Journal* that some fear or nervousness, especially before a race, can be a good thing for reasons other than safety. Nerve cells respond to fear by releasing "certain chemicals and hormones in your body that help you to explode out of the starting gate, move forward at every turn and push through to the finish line. Your nerves are not the enemy—so don't treat them as such. To do your best, you must feel 'some' excitement."[35] The important thing, Perlus emphasizes, is to use visualization or relaxation techniques such as deep breathing to prevent fear from becoming overwhelming.

Although sports psychologists can help athletes develop methods of keeping fear under control, several studies suggest that some individuals will not be as successful as others, because some aspects of adjusting to high-pressure situations are inborn. A study by Debbie Crews at the Mayo Clinic, for instance, found that the brains of golfers who "choke up" and cannot perform well under pressure are different than the brains of golfers who do not do this. Using electrodes to record brain activity, Crews discovered that "chokers" have excess activity in the left side of the brain during stressful competitions. This excess activity interferes with neuron function in the right side of the brain. In non-chokers, activity in both sides of the brain is balanced. Since the left side of the brain controls logic and critical thinking and the right side controls balance and the timing of physical actions, Crews believes the unbalanced brain activity in chokers' brains disrupts both thinking and movement. Visualization and relaxation techniques promote right-brain activity, so she suggests that chokers need more of these therapies than non-chokers to overcome the excessive left-brain activity.

Biology, Experience, and Risk-Taking

Just as some aspects of fear and courage are governed by inborn factors, the same is true of risk-taking behavior. Several studies have found that people who choose to participate in downhill skiing, ski jumping, and freestyle skiing—the riskiest types of skiing—share several personality traits and biological characteristics. Risk-takers tend to be extroverts, like to show off, like to see their desires fulfilled immediately, are naturally self-confident, are good at controlling their emotions, and enjoy seeking out thrilling experiences. While most people who engage in risky sports are careful to train extensively so they can be as safe as possible, some do not seem to care about safety at all. The degree to which individuals enjoy risk-taking and are careless or careful seems to depend partly on inherited genetic factors and partly on experience.

Scientists in Israel were the first to link certain genes to psychological traits such as thrill-seeking. They discovered that variations (minor abnormalities) in a gene called the dopamine receptor-4 gene, which influences the effects of the neurotransmitter dopamine on the brain, are tied to risk-taking and thrill-seeking behavior. Neurotransmitters are brain chemicals that neurons use to communicate with other neurons. Dopamine is important in sending messages that allow movement to occur and in controlling the reward and pleasure centers in the brain. Doctors have determined that people with abnormal dopamine receptor-4 genes may need to engage in risky behaviors to feel pleasure or a sense of well-being.

Other studies indicate that genes associated with the production of the male hormone testosterone also play a role in risk-taking. Young men, who have the highest levels of testosterone, are most likely to be risk-takers. As testosterone levels decline with age, men become less likely to do risky things. Females possess only small amounts of testosterone, and scientists believe this may be why far fewer females are risk-takers.

Other body chemicals that influence risk-taking behavior include a brain enzyme called monoamine oxidase. This enzyme regulates dopamine and other neurotransmitters. People with genes that lead to low levels of monoamine oxidase in the body are likely to be risk-takers and to seek out immediate feelings of pleasure without regard for the consequences. Several genes that regulate the neurotransmitter serotonin, which regulates mood, also affect risk-taking.

> **FRESH POWDER**
>
> **95% vs. 5%**
>
> Proportion of mental vs. physical faculties that sports psychologists say it takes to ski to one's full potential.

An article in *Psychology Today* points out that the genes that promote risk-taking have survived during human evolution because a certain amount of risk-taking can be a positive thing as far as survival of the human species goes. The article states, "Although risk-taking has negative aspects and can even prove fatal, it is a positive force as well. Without risky experiences, humanity would stagnate; there would be little impetus for discovery."[36]

In addition to the genetic influences on risk-taking, experiences such as having friends and family members who engage in risky activities can also affect individual choices. Scientists have determined that about 60 percent of risk-taking is determined by genes and 40 percent by experience. Many people who choose risky sports such as ski jumping do so after being introduced to the sport early in life by family members who enjoy the sport. Young people who later compete in these sports often gain the necessary confidence after gradually learning the necessary skills over a period of years. However, those with genes that promote risk-taking are even likelier to continue in risky sports.

Danger Junkies

For some people, experience and genetic factors can interact to produce another driving force behind risky behavior—addiction. Engaging in risky activities makes some people feel "high" from the release of brain chemicals such as dopamine, norepinephrine (noradrenaline), and endorphins (natural opiate-like chemicals in the body). As

Shane McConkey performs the first ever urban Ski-BASE jump in 2007, off the roof of a hotel in Reno, Nevada.

with addictive drugs, the high can lead some individuals to become danger junkies (sometimes called adrenaline junkies) who crave more and more risky activities. This happens because after a while, the individual no longer feels the high unless he or she receives higher "doses" of danger. Addiction occurs because peoples' bodies habituate, or get used to, a drug or behavior and require more of the substance to achieve the same effects.

Psychologists classify many skiers who thrive on risky behavior as danger junkies. One (now deceased) skier named Shane McConkey is often mentioned as an example. For many years, McConkey skied down the steepest mountains and jumped off enormous cliffs. He often did movie stunts and was widely known for playing James Bond in a 2009 spoof of the movie *The Spy Who Loved Me*. A 2008 article in *Psychology Today* states:

> When you spend decades of your life dropping off cliffs for fun, trying to do something scary enough to produce one's desired high is a bit of a challenge. Which explains why McConkey has added BASE jumping into the equation. BASE jumping is a form of sky-diving off fixed objects. . . . BASE jumping is widely considered the most dangerous sport on earth.[37]

McConkey died in 2009 at age thirty-nine while being filmed BASE jumping in Italy. After his death, many people asked his widow, Sherry, whether she thought Shane should have stopped participating in risky sports. Sherry said in a *Men's Journal* article, "People are constantly asking me how I 'let' Shane do what he did. It just floors me. To me, it would have been like putting an eagle in a cage—a tiny cage."[38]

Other athletes who crave fear and who do not feel alive unless engaged in risky activities echo this sentiment. Canadian freestyle skier Roz Groenewoud, whose teammate Sarah Burke died in a training accident in 2012, said that she wondered whether the risks were worth it after Burke's death. She decided, however, that "life is not any fun without adrenaline rushes. I'd rather be skiing than not skiing, whatever the consequences are."[39]

Whether or not a skier is an extreme risk-taker, one of the most important factors in determining the likelihood of injuries or death is the skier's mastery of skills and technique. Those skiers who devote the most time to training and perfecting their technique not only decrease their chances of injury, but also increase their probability of winning in competition.

CHAPTER 5

Speed Matters: Downhill and Cross-Country Techniques

Just as physical training and mental qualities such as motivation and focus play a big role in determining a skier's success and safety, proper technique is also essential. In downhill and cross-country skiing, where speed is the criterion for winning races, the right techniques allow competitive skiers to achieve maximum speed and endurance while minimizing risks. The author of *Ski Skills* explains that learning proper techniques also allows skiers to ski more efficiently: "The better our technique, the less effort we need to make; subtle movements of our upper body and legs and the correct transference of our weight are far more efficient than laboriously heaving our bodies around bends and over bumps."[40]

Although ski equipment and techniques have changed over the years, the essential technical elements that make skiers into champions remain the same. The book *The Other Side of the Mountain,* which tells the story of 1950s' downhill ski racer Jill Kinmont, for example, describes what Kinmont learned from watching Olympic slalom skiers: "The great lesson Jill learned was that the winners never made little mistakes. No sideslip. No lost motion. They were never lazy for a tenth of a second. . . . A fast finish on every turn, whipping out of the gate already set for the next."[41] These qualities apply in modern times as much as they did when Kinmont was skiing.

Speed Matters

Since the fastest skiers win Alpine and cross-country races, competitors do all they can to control the forces that affect their speed. In Alpine skiing, part of the energy for skiing fast comes from the forces provided by the skier's muscles and part comes from the sloped environment. The Canadian Ski Instructors Alliance explains, "In many sports, speed and forward motion are a result of internal muscular effort. In alpine skiing, gravity provides the pull, and the skier uses movement and muscular effort to influence speed and direction."[42] An important aspect of maximizing speed involves taking advantage of gravity and minimizing the frictional forces that oppose the effects of gravity.

At the start of a downhill course, before skiers begin moving, they possess gravitational potential energy. When they push off and start moving, this potential energy is converted to kinetic energy and momentum. Their speed throughout the course is then determined by the sum of the gravitational energy and muscle energy pushing one way and the opposing forces of friction pushing the other way. However, not all of a skier's muscle energy goes into gaining speed. Physicists have determined that about 56 percent of a skier's muscle energy is spent overcoming the forces of sliding friction and aerodynamic drag. This is why competitive skiers take measures such as using the right skis, ski wax, skintight clothing, and crouching when possible to minimize these frictional forces. By reducing friction, skiers can devote more muscle energy to maximizing speed in other ways that depend on technique. However, experts note that while eliminating some friction is a good thing for ski racers, taking away too much would be disastrous. Physicists estimate that downhill skiers who normally achieve speeds of about 61 miles per hour (99kph) could possibly go 300 miles per hour (482.8kph) if no friction was present. Going this fast would not allow skiers to control their body position or stay on a path. This would result in far more crashes and falls than happen when frictional forces hold the skier back.

Even speeds of about 60 miles per hour (96.5kph) pose extreme challenges to a skier's ability to stay balanced. Thus,

High-Tech Timekeeping

Since winning downhill and cross-country races depends on achieving the fastest time, competitive skiers are always looking for better ways of assessing when and where they are losing fractions of seconds during training and competition. Researchers at the Swedish Winter Sports Research Centre hypothesized that measuring the time elapsed at multiple points on a ski course, rather than just measuring overall time, would give skiers valuable tactical information. They realized, however, that the usual timekeeping methods (stopwatches, photocells, and video cameras) were not accurate enough for this purpose. So they performed experiments in 2011 using a Global Navigation Satellite System (GNSS), which relies on a satellite above Earth to precisely locate objects. GNSS is a type of Global Positioning System (GPS). GPS systems had been used to measure velocity and distance in various sports, but before these experiments, not to gauge intermediate times in a race.

The researchers developed a new GNSS computer program that frequently and accurately measures time elapsed on ski courses. They then placed tiny GPS transmitters in skiers' backpacks to communicate with the GNSS system. The GNSS time measurements during course runs proved to be reliable and accurate. The skiers also found the intermediate time measurements helpful in analyzing their performance. Although the system is expensive, scientists are working on less expensive methods of manufacturing these miniature GPS systems.

it is important for skiers to learn the proper downhill techniques in order to perfect the methods of raising or lowering one's center of gravity and shifting one's weight over the skis to maintain this balance. The center of gravity is the point on the body where the weight above and below are equal. The lower the center of gravity is, the easier it is to stay balanced and maintain speed. This is another reason that skiers often crouch, which lowers their center of gravity. Properly shifting their weight over the skis and bending their knees to absorb the shock of skiing over bumps and valleys also helps skiers balance and stay on track as they ski through the varied terrain on a downhill course.

FRESH POWDER

2

Number of seconds that downhill skiers are in the air after becoming airborne.

Turn, Turn, Turn

One of the biggest challenges to downhill skiers' balance and speed maintenance occurs during the many turns they make to go around curves, so as not to descend a mountain in a dangerously steep straight line. There are several types of turns. Beginners usually execute snowplow or wedge turns, in which skiers turn their skis inward so the tips are closer together than the tails are. This transfers the skiers' weight to the left or right so they can turn in that direction.

A stem turn is appropriate for intermediate skiers and is performed by pointing the ski on the outside of the curve in the direction the skier wishes to turn. For example, to turn right, the skier points the left ski to the right. The skier then transfers his or her weight to the outer ski and points the inner ski in the next turning direction. A series of these motions allows the skier to piece together a string of turns.

Most advanced skiers used parallel turns until the late 1980s. In a parallel turn, skiers bring their feet close together, keeping the skis parallel and leaning in the direction of the turn. This used to be the best and fastest way to maintain the most speed during a turn. With the invention of parabolic, or carving, skis in the late 1980s, however, the faster carved turn became elite skiers' most commonly used turn.

In a carved turn, the skis carve a circle in the snow. The book *Gliding For Gold: The Physics of Winter Sports* explains how a carved turn works:

> The carve turn is driven by the side-cut geometry of the ski. Leaning into the curve and transferring weight to the outer ski causes the ski edge (the inside edge

Elisabeth Goergl performs a carved turn—which makes it easier to control the width of the turn—at a 2009 super-G event.

of the outer ski) to bite the snow. The extra weight forces down the middle of the ski, so that the camber is reversed—the ski bends up at the tip and tail. . . . The carve-turn action, and the shape of the side-cut, means that the ski edge is a circular arc, and so the ski executes a curve by carving a circle in the snow.[43]

Advantages of Carved Turns

Unlike other types of turns, properly executed carved turns barely push aside any snow. Since the speed of a turn is mostly determined by how much snow is sprayed to the sides of the skis, carved turns are therefore faster and slow the skier's progress less than other turns do. This is because energy is required to move snow, and if a skier moves aside a great deal of snow, this takes away energy he or she could otherwise devote to speed. Turns that move aside a lot of snow also slow a skier down considerably because they cause the skis to skid, which reduces the amount of momentum pushing the skier and skis forward. Skidding also increases the amount of sliding friction. Thus, advanced skiers learn to apply weight to the edges of their skis to execute clean carved turns that minimize snow spray. As explained in *The Other Side of the Mountain*: "Snow spraying out from beneath your skis may make a lovely photograph, but it is a sign of unwanted, wasted motion. The same principle holds in diving . . . the better the dive the smaller the splash."[44]

FRESH POWDER

156.2 mph (251.4kph)

World record for the fastest nonmotorized sport on Earth, held by speed skier Simone Origone of Italy.

Besides slowing down skiers less than other turns, carved turns also make it easier for skiers to control the width of a turn. This is because the parabolic shape of carving skis allows a skier's upper body to turn in the same direction the skis are going. With other types of skis, skiers twist the upper body away from the direction of the turn to provide much of the angular momentum (the momentum generated during rotation) that makes the skis turn. With carving skis, however, the parabolic shape provides the force behind the turn, so the body does not have to twist. When the body turns with the skis, it is easier to shift one's weight onto the ski tips to make a turn sharper or onto the tails to make it wider.

While this aspect of carved turns is easier for skiers, the fact that parabolic skis generate more angular momentum than other skis means that the skier ends up exerting additional energy to prevent spinning out of control. With more angular momentum, the centrifugal force that pulls the skier outward on the curve is greater, so they must counteract this force to keep from falling. There are several methods of counteracting centrifugal force. One method is leaning toward the inside of the turn. Another is planting the ski poles in the snow to slow the angular momentum and help balance the body. Still another method is pumping the legs up and down to shift the body's center of gravity to the center of the turning arc.

Whichever methods of control a skier uses, the higher the speed and sharpness of the turn, the more effort is required to maintain balance. This is because the g-force on the body increases with faster changes in position. G-force

Extreme Speed Skiing

Speed skiing, where skiers take a straight line down a steep slope, is an offshoot of downhill ski racing and is the world's fastest nonmotorized sport. It was introduced as a demonstration sport at the 1992 Winter Olympics in Albertville, France, but has never become an Olympic sport. Few ski slopes meet the speed skiing criteria for steepness and smoothness, and experts say this is one reason it is not included in the Olympics.

Speed skiers wear extremely aerodynamic airtight suits and spaceman-like helmets to reduce aerodynamic drag. Speed skiing helmets are teardrop-shaped and cover the skier's head and face. An article in *Popular Science* describes speed skiing suits as "rubberized, polyurethane-coated polypropylene, essentially a skin-tight Ziploc bag for your body." Skiers also wear foam fairings above their boots to further reduce drag and to stabilize their balance. Fairings are sort of like stabilizing flaps on airplane wings. In addition, specially made skis that are wider and longer than most Alpine skis and curved ski poles that hug the skier's body complete speed skiers' maximally aerodynamic package.

John Mahoney. "I'm Sad Speed Skiing Isn't an Olympic Sport." *Popular Science*, February 26, 2010. www.popsci.com/technology/article/2010-02/im-sad-speed-skiing-isnt-olympic-sport.

Speed skiers—such as Linda Baginski, seen here at the FIS Speed Skiing World Cup Final in 2010—must wear extremely aerodynamic suits and helmets.

is a measurement of how much stress impacts the body during acceleration and rotation. A nonmoving person experiences one G due to the earth's gravity. This means gravity pushes against the individual with a force equal to his weight. The g-force on a moving person increases as acceleration increases centrifugal and other forces related to changes in position. At 2 Gs, forces equivalent to twice a a person's weight push against them. Thus, they must exert twice as much muscle energy to counteract these forces. Biomechanics experts say elite skiers often experience up to 3.5 Gs while turning. Staying upright therefore requires significant amounts of muscle energy.

Controlling Those Turns

In addition to leaning, using ski poles, and pumping their legs, skiers also control the forces impacting them during turns by using their boots properly. *The Physics of Skiing* explains, "The boot is the steering wheel for the skis. . . . The skier reacts to gravity and to acceleration and transmits force to the ski through the boot."[45] Ski boots also relay information about the position of the skis to the skier, so the boots must be flexible enough that the skier can feel the skis through them. At the same time, boots must be sturdy enough to support the feet and legs.

Skiers also receive feedback about the position of their skis and about the correctness of their edging and balance skills during turns by studying their ski tracks in the snow. Ideally, snow tracks are thin, clean arcs that resemble curved railroad tracks. If the snow tracks are set too widely apart or show skidding, skiers know they need to work on their weight-shifting and edging skills. Experts say one of the best ways to remedy poor edging and balance skills is by rotating only the legs and feet when initiating a turn. Skiers who also rotate the upper body have difficulty counterbalancing the weight of their feet on the skis' outside edges, and this results in skidding and uneven snow tracks.

For slalom skiers who execute hairpin turns one after another, proper turning techniques are especially important for maintaining the balance and accuracy needed to

Proper turning techniques are essential for slalom skiers such as Mario Matt, seen here at the 2014 Winter Olympics, where he won a gold medal.

complete a race. As an article in the *Journal of Sports Science and Medicine* explains:

> A slalom race consists of two runs with 53 to 70 turning gates per run. With the combination of a complex movement activity and high velocities, it is no surprise that many racers do not finish a course. In 2010, about 30% of women did not finish (DNF) and about 35% of men recorded a DNF in World Cup slalom races.[46]

Slalom skiers keep their turns as close to the turning gates as possible to enhance speed, but getting too close can lead to a DNF if the skier straddles a gate. Missing a gate also results in a DNF. Slalom skiers therefore practice the edging and rotation skills that allow tight, fast, balanced turns over and over to master these techniques.

Cross-Country Techniques

Unlike the turning techniques used in downhill skiing, cross-country skiers usually perform Telemark turns, which require the free-heel bindings that cross-country skiers use. In a Telemark turn, skiers keep their skis parallel. To turn left, they bend the left knee close to the ground, slide the left foot back, and slide the right foot forward. The left ski pole is planted downhill to the skier's left, and the hips, knees, and ankles rotate toward the pole. As with other cross-country techniques, these turns rely mainly on the skier's muscle energy, since the smaller slopes on cross-country courses do not provide much gravitational energy. This is why cross-country skiing is more tiring and requires more endurance than Alpine skiing does, especially since many of the courses span ten or more miles.

The lack of large quantities of gravitational energy means

that the speeds achieved in cross-country skiing are far less than those in downhill as well. Elite cross-country skiers can maintain speeds of 10 to 15 miles per hour (16 to 24kph) for two or more hours, and many literally collapse from exhaustion as they cross the finish line. Studies show that elite cross-country racers going 10 to 15 miles per hour burn nearly 900 calories in an hour. Elite runners running 6 miles per hour (9kph), on the other hand, burn about 775 calories per hour, indicating that cross-country skiers work even harder than distance runners do.

The design of cross-country skis and the use of different types of ski wax minimize friction as much as possible to enhance a skier's energy conservation. As the book *World of Sports Science* explains, cross-country skis "are designed to support the weight of the skier over their greater length, creating efficiency in movement through less resistance against the surface of the snow. The skis are not fixed boards, but each is constructed with a degree of flex, which permits the skier to push off with the foot and receive energy from the ski in return."[47]

Even these features, however, do not negate the fact that cross-country skiing requires more endurance than most other sports.

Classic and Skate Techniques

When cross-country skiers are not turning, they use either the classic or ski skate technique. In the classic technique, skiers move forward with the skis parallel, using a kick-glide motion. In the kick phase, they stand with their knees slightly bent and their body leaning slightly forward. The poles are angled backward. They then apply pressure to the right ski with the right foot while the left arm swings forward with the pole still angled backward. To glide, they shift their weight onto the left ski and move this ski forward while the right arm swings forward and the left arm moves back. The kick-glide sequence continues with the opposing motion of legs and arms. The motion of the ski poles mainly serves to provide extra push and balance.

Many skiers who use the classic technique use kick wax

Stopping and Falling

In addition to learning proper techniques for starting, sliding, and turning, skiers must also learn methods of stopping and falling. On gentle slopes, beginners usually use a wedge stop, also known as a pie or snowplow. Here, skiers put the ski tips together while bending their knees and rotating them inward. According to the authors of *The Physics of Skiing*, "The wedge stance allows the skier to slow the rate of descent because when the skis are flat on the snow their lateral [sideways] skidding generates a plowing force on the outside edges of the skis, which balances the gravity force." More advanced skiers on steeper slopes use a stopping technique called the parallel skid, or skater's stop. The skiers move both skis to a horizontal position across the slope by rotating their body and placing their legs, knees, and feet together. This forces the uphill ski edges to skid.

To fall correctly, ski instructors instruct skiers to sit down or to fall to the side to avoid falling on outstretched hands. If the skis become tangled during a fall, lying on one's back with legs in the air will untangle them. The skier should then roll onto one side and put weight on their knees to stand up.

David Lind and Scott P. Sanders. *The Physics of Skiing*. New York: Springer-Verlag, 2004, p. 95.

to grip the snow so they can glide ahead without slipping. When the snow is extremely icy, skiers may use klister wax, which grips even more than kick wax does. Ski technicians who are part of a competitor's staff carry different types of wax to apply to the skis as snow conditions change.

Ski skaters, in contrast, usually use glide wax under the skis to reduce friction. In the skating style, the skier pushes one ski to the side while gliding forward on the other ski in a motion similar to that used in ice skating. The arms both swing in the same direction, placing the poles in the snow to help push the gliding leg along faster. Skating-style skis are somewhat shorter than those used for the classic technique because ski skaters must pick up one leg during each stride forward.

Because ski skaters use glide wax, and due to the fact that the skating motion puts more energy into each forward glide with less effort, skate skiing tends to be 15 to 25 percent

Hanna Kolb uses the skate skiing technique during the FIS Cross Country World Cup in 2011.

faster than classic style. Studies have also shown that using the skate style works muscles harder and uses more muscles than the classic style does. However, the heart rate of skiers using the classic style goes higher than that of those using the skate style. This indicates that classic-style skiers work the cardiovascular system harder than skate-style skiers do. These results led researchers in a 2011 study to conclude that "from a mechanical and physiological point of view, the skate skiing performance is higher than classical style as a consequence [of] a higher speed with a lower energy cost."[48] Most cross-country skiers learn both techniques because some races require the use of both. In other races, using one or the other technique may be required.

Whichever technique cross-country skiers use, the goal of efficiently using energy to maintain speed and maximize endurance is identical. In contrast, in the cross-country offshoot of ski jumping and in freestyle techniques that include acrobatics, speed and endurance are less central to winning competitions, although they do play a role.

CHAPTER 6

Jumps and Acrobatics: Ski Jumping and Freestyle Techniques

Although downhill skiing is considered to be a risky sport, many experts consider ski jumping and freestyle skiing to be the most "extreme" forms of the sport that attract the most risk-takers. Proper technique can literally mean the difference between life and death for skiers in these styles that include flying through the air or performing acrobatics while airborne.

Ski Jumping

Actual ski jumping events are far different than the short jumps that downhill skiers take while navigating a slope. Ski jumpers jump from one specially constructed hill onto the slope of a smaller hill. There are three categories of competitive ski jumping: the normal hill, which is 278 feet 10 inches to 357 feet 7 inches (85 to 109m) tall with a K-point (expected jumping distance) of 262 to 328 feet (80 to 100m); the large hill, which is 360 feet 10 inches (110m) or more with a K-point of 393 to 459 feet (120 to 130m); and ski flying, which is 606 feet 11 inches (185m) tall with a K-point of

606 feet 11 inches. There are only five ski-flying hills in the world, and it is a World Cup sport but not an Olympic sport.

Each jumper is allowed three jumps in competition. The first is a practice jump, and the scores of the second and third are added together. A jumper receives 60 points for landing at the designated K-point and extra points for exceeding this distance. The number of extra points depends on the hill. At the 2010 Winter Olympics in Vancouver, Canada, for example, 1.8 points were added for each additional meter beyond the K-point in the large hill jump. Two points were added for each meter beyond the normal hill K-point. Points are deducted if the jumper does not reach the K-point. Each judge can also award up to 20 points for technique and style. These points depend on the skier's body position during each jumping phase. Judges may also adjust points in situations where weather conditions such as wind impact jumpers.

Usually, the winning jumpers receive the highest scores for both distance and style. However, sometimes this is not

Ski flyer Bjorn Einar Romoren—seen here at the 2006 Winter Olympics—held the record for longest jump (784 feet) from 2005 to 2011.

FRESH POWDER

100–200 yards (91.44–182.88m)

Length many elite ski jumpers fly.

the case. At the 2010 Winter Olympics, for example, the gold medalist in the normal hill, Simon Ammann of Switzerland, did not receive high scores for style, but got an extra 7.2 points for jumping record-breaking distances of 344 and 354 feet (105 and 108m). Currently, the longest recorded ski jumping distance is 809 feet (246.5m), achieved in 2011 by the Norwegian ski jumper Johan Remen Evensen.

Ski Jumping Phases

Each ski jump contains four phases. The first is the inrun phase. To get to the inrun, skiers ride an elevator to a scaffold, or tower, at the top of the jumping hill. They prepare to ski down the 10-foot (3m) inrun area by crouching with their arms held backward to reduce aerodynamic drag. They then ski to the end of the inrun on skis that are as long as cross-country skis but twice as wide, and begin the takeoff phase where they launch themselves into the air.

The takeoff technique and speed both influence the jump distance. Olympic jumpers take off at speeds of 55 to 65 miles per hour (88 to 104kph). According to a 2012 study in the *Journal of Human Kinetics,* the takeoff phase involves several complex moves that seek to maximize speed and jumping height: "During the take-off, a ski jumper has to solve five relatively independent motor tasks: the energy of the take-off, aerodynamics, accuracy, optimal angular momentum and arm movement."[49] When the jumpers jump, they try to create the maximum upward momentum by raising their center of gravity as high as possible, so they jump from a crouching position. Most of the power for the jump comes from the knees, upper legs, and hips. The jumpers, however, do not extend their body straight up during the jump, as this would add aerodynamic drag and decrease the takeoff speed. Instead, they hold their body at a 7- to 12-degree angle, keeping their chest low while extending their legs straight

down and holding the skis horizontal to maximize the height of the jump.

During the next phase, the free-flight phase, the jumpers fly as far as possible, often at heights reaching 100 feet (30m). The body position and the position of the skis, as well as the skiers' weight, all affect the distance flown. Athletes who weigh less fly farther, and many competitive ski jumpers deliberately lose weight to help their scores. In fact, numerous instances of dangerously thin, anorexic jumpers led the International Ski Federation and the International Olympic Committee to institute regulations that disqualify jumpers whose body mass index is less than 21.

Johan Clarey is seen at the inrun phase of his ski jump during a training session before the 2014 Winter Olympics.

Physicists have determined that the critical components of the body and ski positions are the angle between the skis and the direction of travel, the angle between the skier's legs and the skis, the angle between the skier's legs and torso, and the angle between the skis. The ideal angles for all these components of a jump are those that reduce drag and increase aerodynamic lift.

SKI JUMPING

To maximize lift and reduce air drag, ski jumpers need to optimize the angle of the skis and the direction of movement (~40°), the angle of the legs above the skis (~60°), and the angle of the legs and torso (~160°).

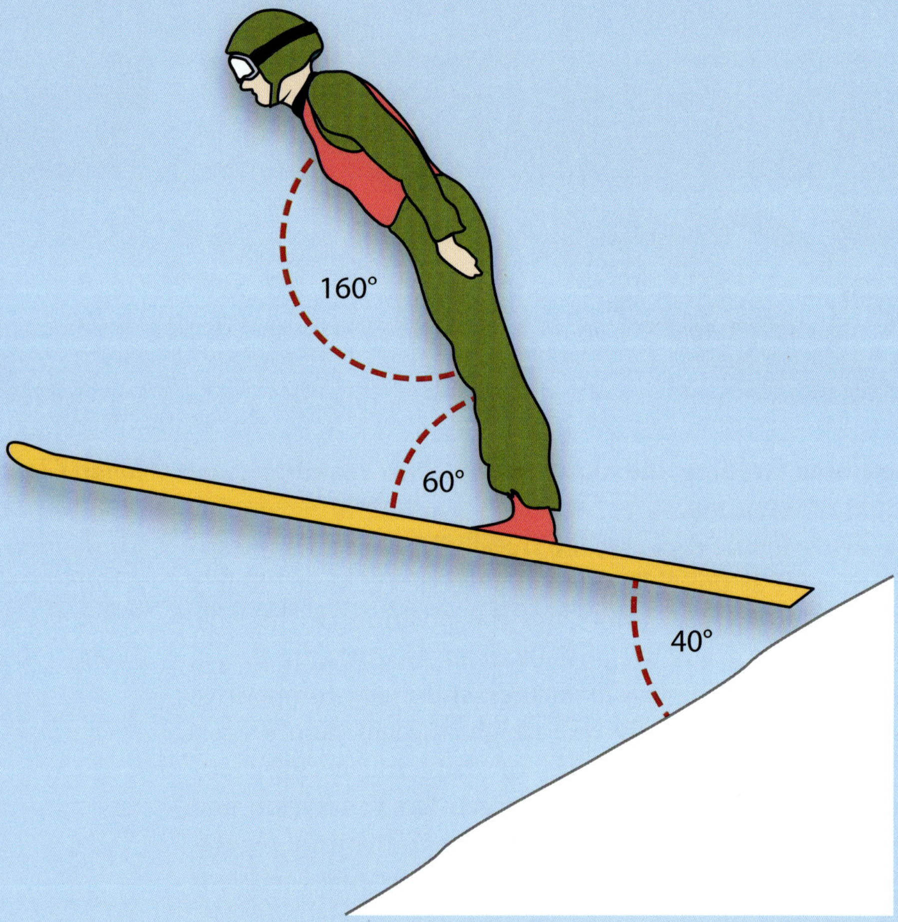

Like aerodynamic drag, aerodynamic lift depends on the size and speed of a moving object. However, while drag pulls an object in the direction opposite to the way it is moving, the direction in which lift acts depends on an object's shape and angle of incline. The most familiar shape and angle that make the force of lift act in an upward direction is an airplane wing set in a horizontal direction. Through trial and error, ski jumpers discovered that leaning the body far forward with the skis held in a V shape provides the most aerodynamic lift

Ski Jumping and Anorexia

Because weighing less helps ski jumpers jump farther, some jumpers develop eating disorders such as anorexia to gain a competitive edge. In fact, studies found that more than 20 percent of the ski jumpers at the 2002 Olympics were seriously underweight. Kinesiology experts estimate that losing 2.2 pounds (1kg) can add 6 to 13 feet (2 to 4m) to jumping distance.

In 2004 the International Ski Federation (FIS) implemented new rules to discourage jumpers from being dangerously underweight, but this has not eliminated the problem. In 2010, for example, Martin Schmitt of Germany became exhausted and had to leave the World Cup competition because of his unhealthy weight. The 5 foot 11 inch tall Schmitt weighed about 138 pounds (63kg) and was reportedly consuming only about 1,300 calories per day. Doctors say this type of severe caloric restriction can lead to heart failure and other serious health problems.

Even though many jumpers are still underweight, Alan Alborn of the U.S. team said in a 2010 *Sports Illustrated* article that the FIS rules have improved matters. He pointed out that many of his teammates on the 1998, 2002, and 2006 Olympic teams "were hardly eating at all, and there was a lot of appetite suppression going on, with guys smoking, chewing tobacco, doing everything they could to keep their appetite under control. . . . The guys who are jumping today may seem light compared to the average person, but I think they're much healthier than they used to be."

Quoted in Phil Taylor. "Battle to Remain Abnormally Lean Touchy Subject in Ski Jumping." *Sports Illustrated*, February 16, 2010. http://sportsillustrated.cnn.com/2010/olympics/2010/writers/phil_taylor/02/16/skinny.ski.jumpers/index.html.

in ski jumping. This is because these configurations block the flow of air around them the least amount, so the air can push the skier upward.

Ski jumpers originally held their skis parallel to each other during free-flight. In the early 1980s, however, the Polish jumper Miroslaw Graf pioneered a new technique called the V-style. In 1985, the Swedish jumper Jan Boklov began using the V-style, and some historians credit Boklov with inventing it, while others credit Graf. Some call the V-style the Graf-Boklov style.

Ski jumpers who used the V-style in the 1980s were penalized by judges who considered it to be bad form. By the 1990s, however, the style was accepted as superior to the parallel style and it is used almost exclusively today. Physicists proved that the V-style creates about 28 percent more lift than the parallel style and leads to a 10 percent increase in jumping distance. Studies have also shown that the ideal V-angle for maximizing lift is 30 degrees. According to an article in *Proceedings: International Symposium for Olympic Research*, this V-angle "allowed jumpers to use the air much like an airplane wing."[50]

Other Influences on Flight

Physics experiments have also determined the ideal angles for the other critical components of the free-flight phase. For instance, many studies have found that the best angle between the skis and the direction of travel is 30 to 40 degrees. Physicists and biomechanics experts call this angle the angle of attack. However, other studies indicate that the angle of attack should change throughout the flight path to maximize jumping distance. Physicist Mark Denny writes: "A small initial angle of attack serves to reduce drag, and a later large angle of attack increases lift. . . . Drag increases pretty much proportionally with the angle of attack, whereas lift increases and then falls away."[51] The ideal angles for the body parts can also change with the flight path, so elite jumpers learn to slightly adjust their body and ski positions during the course of the free-flight.

The Evolution of Ski Jumping Techniques

Ski jumping techniques have changed over the years to help jumpers achieve greater distances. The first known ski jumper, the Norwegian military officer Olaf Rye, jumped 31 feet 2 inches (9.5m) in 1809. Historians believe he used the Optrakke style that became common among people in the Norwegian countryside. In this style, the skier bent the knees and upper body slightly before taking off from a slope or rooftop. After jumping, the skier straightened his or her body and pulled his or her feet up close to the body while flying.

In the early 1900s, jumpers began using the stretch-forward style to make their bodies more aerodynamic while airborne. Several variations on this style developed. The Norwegian jumpers Tullin Thams and Sigmund Ruud developed the Kongsberger technique, where the jumper added a large hip bend to the forward lean of the body. In the Bradl style pioneered by the Austrian Sepp Bradl, the jumper stretched his or her arms forward rather than moving them back and forth as was typical in other techniques. In 1936, Bradl was the first ski jumper to exceed 328 feet (100m); he jumped 331 feet (101m).

In the 1950s, Swiss jumper Andreas Daescher discovered that holding the arms close to the body in a backward direction significantly reduced aerodynamic drag, so he introduced the Daescher style. This was also known as the parallel style because it included holding the skis parallel to each other. This style predominated until the V-style became popular in the late 1980s.

Another factor that can influence drag and lift is altitude. The higher up the location is, the thinner the air and the less drag and lift it imposes. The reduced air density and pressure at high altitudes reduce drag and lift by about 3 percent for every 1,000 feet (304.8m) of altitude. For example, at

FRESH POWDER

809 ft 8 in (246.5m)

World record for longest ski jump.

4,921 feet (1,500m), an object experiences about 15 percent less drag and lift than at sea level. This means that a ski jumper will fly farther but lower at the higher altitude.

Competitors therefore learn to compensate. "Elite athletes are able to adapt their flight style to thin air conditions in order to maximize jump length and to keep the flight stable,"[52] explains a study in the *Journal of Biomechanics*. At high altitudes, jumpers change their body position so as to reduce drag at takeoff and increase it at the end of the flight so they stay in the air longer and can fly farther. They achieve this by changing the body angle relative to the skis, which biomechanics experts call the beta angle. The beta angle at higher altitudes needs to be greater than the one lower down to compensate for less lift and drag, so jumpers do not lean the body as far forward at any time during free-flight when high up. One study found that the average beta angle for Olympic ski jumpers was 16.1 degrees at high altitudes compared to 11.7 degrees at lower ones.

Landing and Outrun

After a jumper manipulates his flight path to make the free-flight phase carry him as far as possible, the landing phase, followed by the jumper sliding to a finish on a gently sloping outrun area, begins. The landing area consists of hard-packed snow, so landings are not soft. However, the jumper's speed is low by this time since jumping hills are designed so their slope tapers off to match the skier's expected place and angle of landing. Therefore, the impact on the jumper is not strong. Physicists have determined that the ground reaction forces experienced when a jumper lands near the K-point are about the same as when someone lands after jumping off a 1.5-foot (.5m) platform. Although jumpers seek to exceed the K-point to obtain higher scores, jumping farther increases the ground reaction forces and the risk of injuries. This is because when jumpers land past the K-point, the slope where they land is not tapered to match their angle of approach and they land harder. Another factor that affects the landing impact is the wind. According to a 2009 study, "Wind blowing up the hill increases the jump length dramatically and decreases the landing velocity, which eases the landing, and vice versa for wind from behind."[53]

Ski jumpers land with their knees bent to absorb the landing forces, both for safety reasons and style points. Bending a moving body part absorbs external forces because bending increases the time and distance over which the body part slows down. Increasing the time and distance decreases the ground reaction forces when a jumper lands, just as a car bumper that bends absorbs some of the forces of a crash so there is less chance of passengers being injured.

The correct landing style also helps skiers maintain their balance and distribute their weight evenly so both legs can cushion the impact. The body position while they are airborne in the free-flight phase is one factor that influences their ability to land correctly. If the body is properly aligned and does not lean to one side during free-flight, it is much easier for the jumper to make a straight, balanced landing. Ideally, during the landing the skier's head is angled in front of his or her hips, directly over the knees. Ski jumping rules also require jumpers to land in the Telemark position, with one leg in front of the other as the knees bend low to the ground. Failure to land in this position or to stay balanced and upright results in lost points.

Aerial Freestyle

While most competitive ski jumpers experience low landing forces, studies show that freestyle aerialists experience landing forces equivalent to jumping from a 20-foot-tall (60m) building. Even though ski jumpers travel at twice the speed and fall twice as far, aerialists' landings are significantly more forceful because ski jumpers "are flying close to the hill which is shaped for their flight trajectory,"[54] states a NASA study. Aerialists, on the other hand, go farther out from the hill so they can include acrobatics while they fall. However, even with these large landing forces, aerialists

At the 2014 Winter Olympics, Anton Kushnir participates in qualifying freestyle skiing aerials, one of the most technically challenging sports.

rarely injure themselves upon landing because they land in deep, soft snow that is never packed or groomed.

Aerial competitors jump off snow-covered metal or wooden structures and perform gymnastics-like somersaults and twists before landing on a landing hill. Judges award points based on the quality of the takeoff, jumping form, landing, and degree of acrobatic difficulty. According to the Freestyle Ski Acrobatique organization:

> Aerials is one of the most technically challenging and spectator-captivating sports in the world. At the World Cup level, competitors hit the jump, or 'kickers,' at speeds of 60 km/h [37.3 mph] or faster, launch themselves some 20 meters [65.6 feet] in the air and perform up to three back somersaults with as many as five twists, touching down on a landing hill so steep that most people would be nervous just skiing down it.[55]

Each competitor performs two jumps that must vary by one somersault or one twist.

The main principle of physics that governs aerial moves is the conservation of angular momentum. The skier's angular momentum is determined by how much the skier rotates his or her body during the takeoff. The skiers can harness energy to generate this angular momentum in several ways. They can use ground reaction forces to push themselves into a twist or turn during the takeoff, or they can circle their hips as though they were using a Hula-Hoop. This is called hula twisting. Another method of generating energy is the tilt method. Here, skiers move their arms up and down or forward and backward to tilt their body to one side. Sometimes aerialists use a combination of methods.

Moving the arms and legs also affects the speed of the acrobatics and the speed at which the force of gravity pushes the skier down. Raising the arms on the launch ramp to raise the center of mass slows the speed of the fall, and moving the arms or legs outward slows the speed of the twists and flips. Tucking the arms or legs inward conserves angular momentum, so it increases the speed of the acrobatics.

Learning to accurately move the body and skis to perform these acrobatics and to land safely requires a great deal of practice that develops excellent balance, agility, flexibility, power, and strength. In addition, freestyle experts emphasize that aerialists must first become expert downhill skiers before they can master aerial acrobatics. After that, they enroll in a certified freestyle training course and use a trampoline to practice their flips and twists. Many ski resorts

Women and Ski Jumping

The 2014 Winter Olympics in Sochi, Russia, were the first to include female ski jumpers. In the past, the International Olympic Committee argued that too few female ski jumpers existed to justify allowing them to compete in the Olympics. However, in a 2010 journal article, kinesiologist John Gleaves of Pennsylvania State University argued that gender bias was actually responsible for this policy. Gleaves pointed out that in Scandinavia, women traditionally were discouraged from ski jumping because it was considered a "manly" sport. He stated that this led the International Ski Federation to exclude female ski jumpers from elite competitions and to deny them adequate training and support. Like many others who supported efforts to include women's ski jumping in the Olympics, Gleaves believed these policies sent a prejudicial message. He wrote, "In instances where no biological or physiological reasons exist for such inequalities, women ought to compete in the same type of events as men. Whether intentional or not, such disparity in the events provides the appearance that women are inferior athletes." Gleaves also pointed out that since women tend to be smaller and lighter than men, they are actually better suited for competitive ski jumping.

John Gleaves. "Too fit to fly: how female Nordic ski jumping challenges the IOC's approach to gender equality." *Proceedings: International Symposium for Olympic Research*, Annual 2010, p. 278.

also provide water ramps where aerialists can practice their moves and safely fall into a pool of water.

Moguls Moves

Like aerial freestylists, moguls skiers need to develop excellent balance and other physical qualities along with being competent downhill skiers before they can master moguls. Moguls take place on sloped trails with many man-made

Gold medalist Jonny Moseley participates in the 1998 Winter Olympics. Skiers use their legs like shock absorbers as they go over each mogul.

bumps, or moguls, and valleys. The course can range from 656 to 885 feet (200 to 270m), with each mogul set about 11.5 feet (3.5m) apart. In addition to maneuvering around or over the moguls, competitors make two jumps that include acrobatic tricks. Moguls rules mandate that while executing these jumps, the skier's upper body must face straight down the hill and the lower body and skis must turn constantly in spins, flips, or ski-grabbing moves. "Turn" judges award points for speed and turning techniques on the ground, and "air" judges rate the quality and difficulty of the

Sarah Burke

One freestyle skier who was instrumental in getting the superpipe event accepted into the 2014 Olympics was Sarah Burke of Canada. Burke died in January 2012 at age twenty-nine after sustaining a head injury while training in Utah. She was the first competitive female freestyle skier to earn medals in four Winter X Games. After her death, Canadian Freestyle Team CEO Peter Judge stated in a *USA Today* article, "Sarah, in many ways, defines the sport. She's been involved since the very, very early days as one of the first people to bring skis into the pipe."

Burke not only trained hard to perfect her technique, but also took time to teach freestyle classes for children and to mentor young competitors. She was a registered organ donor, and upon her death, her organs saved and improved the lives of many recipients.

Quoted in "Canadian Freestyle Skier Sarah Burke Dies at 29." *USA Today*, January 19, 2012. http://usatoday30.usatoday.com/sports/olympics/story/2012-01-19/freestyle-skier-sarah-burke-death/52680120/1.

acrobatics. Top moguls skiers maneuver past approximately four bumps per second, but the fastest competitors do not always win. In fact, going too fast over these bumps causes many skiers to fall. To keep one's speed under control, moguls champion Jonny Moseley recommends, "Don't let the mogul push your feet: Actively suck them up. Jump before you get to the crest of a mogul, pull your feet up and over, land softly and high on the backside then skid to dump speed."[56]

Several principles of physics and biomechanics govern moguls techniques. As in downhill skiing, the forces of friction, drag, gravity, and ground reaction forces act on moguls skiers, and as in aerials, the forces of angular momentum and gravity govern mogulists' acrobatic moves and landings.

To control the effects of gravity, moguls skiers bend and straighten their legs to act like shock absorbers as they ski over each mogul. By crouching on the high areas and standing up straight on the low ones, they change their center of gravity to keep the ground reaction forces constant. This keeps the skier's center of gravity moving in a straight line. Keeping the center of mass moving in a straight line minimizes the forces acting on the skier, so he or she will experience less jarring from acceleration, as explained by Newton's second law. This helps the skier stay balanced.

Other Types of Freestyle

While aerials and moguls are the best-known types of freestyle skiing, several other types exist. At the 2014 Winter

Olympics, two additional styles debuted—ski superpipe and slopestyle. Before these two freestyles were accepted into the Olympics, they were part of the Winter X Games. Ski superpipe grew out of surfers, skateboarders, and snowboarders doing acrobatic tricks in large storm drains. Ski superpipers perform in 22-foot-tall (6.7m) pipes. Slopestyle uses a ski course called a terrain park that contains numerous obstacles such as rails, tables, and jumping platforms. It developed from similar terrain parks used by skateboarders

Joffrey Pollet-Villard competes in superpipe—the most dangerous of all the freestyle events—at the 2013 European Winter X Games.

and BMX bikers. Many ski resorts are starting to add terrain parks for recreational and competitive slopestylers.

Superpipe and slopestyle athletes sustain more injuries and deaths than those in other freestyle events, and this has led to controversies about safety. After Canadian superpipe champion Sarah Burke died in a 2012 training accident, many health experts voiced concerns about these sports. Freestyle skiers, however, seem to accept the risks and rarely back away after sustaining injuries. As Burke stated in a 2010 *USA Today* interview, "I've been very lucky with the injuries I've had. It's part of the game. Everybody gets hurt."[57]

CHAPTER 7

The Slippery Slope: Skiing Injuries

Skiing is considered to be a risky sport due to high speeds, jumping on and off steep slopes, and bitterly cold weather. Doctors treat hundreds of thousands of skiing injuries each year. The area of medicine dedicated to the prevention and treatment of sports injuries is called sports medicine. Most sports medicine doctors are specialists in orthopedic surgery. Other professionals such as physical and occupational therapists, athletic trainers, and sports psychologists also play a role in this area of health care. Physical therapists help athletes recover from injuries and surgeries by manipulating and exercising patients' muscles. An occupational therapist is are a type of rehabilitation specialist who helps patients relearn or develop new ways of performing everyday activities such as eating and dressing. Sports psychologists help athletes recover from injuries by motivating them to pursue aggressive rehabilitation and by assisting them with overcoming fears of reinjury if they choose to continue the sport.

The doctors who wrote the book *Winter Sports Medicine Handbook* emphasize that "the most effective sports medicine practitioners not only understand the medical problems encountered in active people but understand their sport as well."[58] By understanding the sport, doctors and therapists are aware of athletes' need to rehabilitate certain

FRESH POWDER

Women sustain more skiing injuries than men each year.

abilities and physical attributes. Thus, many professionals who treat skiers are also avid skiers themselves.

Skiing Injuries

The number of skiing injuries has risen dramatically in recent years, mostly because many more people now ski. Most experts believe that skiing has actually become safer due to improvements in skis, boots, and bindings. The risks of injury are three to five times higher for beginners than for elite skiers, in large part because many beginners try to ski faster than they should on steeper slopes than they are ready to tackle. Elite skiers, however, also experience many injuries. The United States Consumer Product Safety Commission reports that doctors treated more than 144,000 snow skiing injuries in the United States alone in 2010. There are also an average of 40 to 50 deaths from ski injuries each year in the United States. The latest FIS (International Ski Federation) Injury Surveillance System (2006–2009), which tracks injuries among World Cup skiers, reports 35.5 injuries per 100 athletes per season for Alpine, 44.6 for freestyle, 20.3 for ski jumping, and 11.4 for cross-country.

The American College of Sports Medicine states that 75 to 85 percent of ski injuries result from falls, 11 to 20 percent from collisions with objects or other skiers, and 2 to 9 percent from malfunctioning ski lifts. Many of these injuries occur when a skier is tired after hours of skiing. Researchers have found that fatigue leads to errors in posture and judgment that make injuries more likely. Fatigue in muscles also results in biological changes that promote injuries. Investigators in a 2011 study on Alpine skiers who skied for more than three hours write, "Prolonged submaximal or maximal muscle contractions affect the capacity of muscles to generate forces and alters muscle activity."[59] Doctors measure muscle activity with a machine called an electromyograph, which records electrical activity in muscle fibers. When a muscle becomes fatigued, it recruits more FT (fast twitch) fibers to allow the muscle to continue to

Jill Kinmont

In 1955, eighteen-year-old Jill Kinmont broke her neck in a catastrophic fall on Rustler Mountain in Salt Lake City, Utah, during a qualifying race for the 1956 Winter Olympics. Her injuries left her a quadriplegic. The fall occurred the same week that *Sports Illustrated* magazine featured Kinmont on its cover as an up-and-coming American skier.

The 1966 book *The Other Side of the Mountain* and the 1974 movie of the same title tell the true story of Kinmont's life before and after the accident. Although she was paralyzed below the neck, Kinmont resolved to live a fulfilling life. The book notes that "Jill was grateful that she had been forced to look beyond her small, bright little world of competitive skiing, to notice and begin to care about a broader universe."

During months of grueling physical therapy, she learned to operate her own wheelchair, feed herself, and create paintings. She also fought to obtain admission to college at UCLA in an era when accommodations for the disabled were nonexistent. Once she was admitted, Kinmont began tutoring elementary school students and decided to become a teacher, despite the fact that most teaching programs would not accept disabled people. She finally obtained her teaching credential at the University of Washington and later taught underprivileged children in her home state of California. She also married truck driver John Boothe and the couple adopted a daughter. After Jill's death in 2012, many friends said that what they most remembered about her was the always present smile on her face.

E.G. Valens. *The Other Side of the Mountain*. New York: Harper & Row, 1966, p. 243.

generate power, and muscle activity therefore increases. As muscle activity increases, the muscles lose more and more of the glycogen they use for energy, and fatigue increases even more. With less energy to devote to power and balance, the chance of injuries of all types grows.

The Most Common Injuries

The most common ski injuries are head trauma, broken bones (fractures), sprains, dislocated joints, and scrapes and other skin injuries from falls. Many times, particularly in Alpine and freestyle skiing, skiers experience multiple

FRESH POWDER

1/2

Proportion of all skiing injuries that are knee injuries.

injuries on one or more occasions. For instance, Australian aerialist Alisa Camplin suffered two broken ankles, nine concussions, a broken collarbone, a broken hand, a separated shoulder, torn knee ligaments, a torn Achilles tendon, and numerous broken ribs during her aerials career in the late 1990s and early 2000s. Ski racer and coach Dave McCoy broke his leg in twenty-eight places at the Sugar Bowl competition in 1942 and was not able to ski again for four years. McCoy's student Jill Kinmont became a quadriplegic in 1955 after breaking her back and numerous other bones.

While most skiing injuries are not fatal, the *Canadian Medical Association Journal* reports that "Traumatic brain injury is the leading cause of death and catastrophic injury among those who ski."[60] For this reason, many countries require skiers to wear helmets, which reduce the chances of sustaining serious head injuries. One event that spurred helmet requirements in many places was the 2009 death of actress Natasha Richardson, who was not wearing a helmet when she fell and sustained an epidural hematoma (bleeding in the brain) during a ski lesson in Quebec, Canada.

About 20 percent of skiing injuries involve the head, neck, or spine; 30 to 40 percent are to the upper limbs; and 55 percent are to the legs. While most leg injuries used to involve broken bones, with today's stiffer, more supportive boots and releasable bindings, the majority of leg injuries are ligament and tendon injuries in the knees from falls or from overusing and over-fatiguing the knee joints. The most common knee injury is to the medial collateral ligament (MCL), which connects the femur and tibia bones. Most MCL injuries are sprains, where the ligament twists and sometimes tears when forces are applied to the outer side of the knee while the knee is bent. MCL sprains usually heal with rest, ice, and elevation, but sometimes require surgery.

Another common knee injury is tearing the anterior cruciate ligament (ACL). This most often happens when the stiff back of a ski boot, along with a twisting ski tail, apply

Marie-Michele Gagnon warms up—which reduces the risk of injury—during an Alpine skiing training session before the 2014 Winter Olympic Games.

enough pressure to tear the ligament during a fall. About half of ACL ruptures require surgery, and rehabilitating the knee after surgery often takes six or more months. Athletes therefore dread ACL injuries.

The most common upper-limb skiing injury is sprains or tears in the ulnar collateral ligament in the thumb. This ligament connects bones in the metacarpophalangeal joint at the thumb's base, where it prevents the thumb from bending sideways. Like most other arm, hand, and shoulder injuries, these ligament injuries usually occur when skiers put out their arms to break a fall while still holding the ski poles. The thumb is pulled outward, resulting in ligament damage or in broken bones. Many of these injuries require surgery to restore the thumb's mobility.

Since all of these skiing injuries are painful and can cause disability or even death, sports medicine experts emphasize injury prevention. One of the most important preventive measures skiers can take is performing adequate conditioning and fitness training. Although being fit does not eliminate the risk of injuries, it does reduce the risk, because fit athletes have better endurance and balance. When injuries do occur, those who are physically fit also tend to recover faster.

Other preventive measures include warming up the muscles before skiing and using equipment that is the right

Alisa Camplin competes in the 2006 Winter Olympics, where she won a bronze medal. She had a complete knee reconstruction after an accident in 2002.

size and type for a particular kind of skiing. Experts also recommend that people take lessons before attempting to ski and that they only ski on slopes that match their level of experience. Ski instructors teach skiers to watch out for rocks, patches of ice, and obstacles such as trees. They also teach the correct methods of turning, stopping, and using body parts in skiing techniques.

Rehabilitation and Safety

When prevention fails to stop an injury, sometimes skiers cannot ski again if the injury is serious enough or if fear of reinjury prevents them from participating. However, many athletes, especially elite competitors, go to great lengths to get back into shape so they can continue to compete. After winning an Olympic gold medal in 2002, for example, Alisa Camplin tore her ACL for the second time while attempting a quadruple twisting double somersault during train-

Doping and Skiing

One health issue that affects all major sports is doping, which some athletes engage in to enhance their performance. Doping can involve the use of strength- or energy-enhancing drugs such as steroids or amphetamines (stimulants), or the use of medical techniques such as unnecessary blood transfusions to improve one's oxygen-carrying capability. Blood doping can also involve taking drugs that stimulate the body to produce red blood cells.

Doping has been banned in all amateur and competitive sports, including skiing, since it endangers athletes' lives and can give them unfair advantages. Steroids, for instance, bulk up muscles, but have dangerous side effects such as kidney failure and immune system damage. Another reason for banning doping, states the International Ski Federation, is that "Anti-doping programmes seek to preserve what is intrinsically valuable about sport. This intrinsic value is often referred to as 'the spirit of sport.'" If athletes are caught doping or if they refuse screening tests, they are disqualified from competition and may be stripped of any medals won.

Skiing has seen its share of doping cases. For example, in 2002, members of Finland's men's cross-country Olympic ski team were disqualified for blood doping. In 2006, Russian skier Olga Pyleva lost her silver Olympic medal when blood tests revealed stimulant drugs, and in 2009, the International Olympic Committee fined the Austrian Olympic Committee $1 million for covering up doping by four Austrian skiers.

International Ski Federation. "Introduction." *FIS Anti-Doping Rules*, 2013 Edition, p. 6. www.fis-ski.com/mm/Document/documentlibrary/Medical/02/04/20/fis-anti-doping-rules-2013_Neutral.pdf.

ing. After surgery, which included a complete knee reconstruction, she worked tirelessly with her coaches, physical therapists, and sports psychologist to prepare for the 2006 Winter Olympics. She won a bronze medal at the Olympics and considered it to be her greatest accomplishment, stating in a news article, "This is so much better than the first time round because I've gone through so much heartbreak. It feels like magic."[61]

Camplin credits her coaches, medical doctors, and sports psychologist with keeping her unique needs and desires in mind while helping her recover. Studies have shown that athletes who address both physical and psychological issues have the best chances of making complete recoveries. However, a 2011 study found that the most important aspect of recovery is the quality of the physical therapy an athlete receives. The researchers write, "Well-planned and carefully conducted physical therapy is a significant element of treatment, because it allows one to return to practicing sport safely and in a relatively short time."[62]

While many skiers accept the risks inherent in skiing and are willing to work hard to overcome their injuries, some have spoken out about the need for international skiing federations to make all types of skiing safer. Canadian Alpine ski racer Kelly VanderBeek, for instance, expressed this view at a safety summit after she fractured and tore ligaments in her knee in 2009 and was unable to compete in the 2010 World Cup and Olympics. VanderBeek said, "The equipment and the speeds have gotten to a point where, the way we create G-force in a turn, is beyond the capabilities of the human body and we're unable to sustain those speeds and those forces. When something goes wrong, it goes really wrong."[63]

Many sports medicine experts agree with this assessment, and some have suggested that restrictions on certain ski waxes be implemented to prevent overly fast speeds. Others have recommended that the increasingly common practice of injecting water into ski course snow to make it slicker should stop. Organizations such as FIS, however, have resisted most efforts to slow skiers down because they say the exact way in which excessive speed causes injuries should be thoroughly investigated first. They also point out that most skiers do not want to slow down. For instance, many experts who contributed to a 2010 study by the University of Salzburg in Austria blamed carving skis for increases in speed-related injuries, but noted that skiers were not likely to stop using them.

Cold Weather–Related Medical Problems

While many skiing injuries result from falls and collisions, even more medical problems each year are associated with the cold skiing environment. For example, many skiers develop exercise-induced bronchospasm (EIB), which is a condition similar to asthma. In EIB, cold weather combined with vigorous exercise causes the bronchial tubes to narrow. Scientists believe EIB occurs when cold, dry air dries out and inflames cells in the lungs. EIB makes breathing difficult, and while people with asthma are more susceptible, anyone can develop it. Sports doctors estimate that 15 to 50 percent of Winter Olympics athletes suffer from EIB at some point. Treatment, if needed, consists of drugs that open the airways.

Hermann Maier wears protection against the cold while competing in extreme weather conditions at a 2006 race in Lake Louis, Canada, where the temperature was 5⁰ F (-15⁰ Celsius.)

Other cold-related medical problems can often be avoided by dressing properly while skiing. Snow blindness, for instance, which occurs when unprotected eyes are exposed to the sun's ultraviolet rays being reflected off the snow, can be prevented by wearing ski goggles with side-shields. Snow blindness leads to severe eye pain and impaired vision, and sometimes the damage is permanent.

Wearing warm, dry clothing and covering as much of the skin as possible can often prevent several skin conditions caused by exposure to cold temperatures. One of these is chilblains, which involves the inflammation of blood vessels in the skin, usually on the face, hands, or feet after long-term exposure to cold. Another is frostnip, where the outer skin layers freeze and become white, hardened, and numb. When deeper tissue layers freeze, the condition is called frostbite. Rewarming the skin with warm water can be painful but effective in treating these conditions. If the tissue stays frozen long enough, however, it may have to be cut out or a limb may have to be amputated to eliminate dead tissue.

The most serious cold weather–related medical issue is hypothermia. Here, the body temperature drops below 95°F (36.5°C). When cells in the body cool too much or freeze, they cannot work properly. This is especially dangerous and can be fatal if cells in the heart get cold enough to produce abnormal heartbeats known as cardiac arrhythmias. Symptoms of hypothermia may include dizziness; mental confusion; uncontrollable shivering; rigid muscles; dark, puffy skin; and unconsciousness. Treatment usually consists of rewarming the entire body with blankets and performing cardiopulmonary resuscitation (CPR) if necessary.

Physics and Hypothermia

Hypothermia is caused by the body losing heat. This can happen by any of the three processes of conduction, convection, or radiation. Conduction occurs when two objects with different temperatures touch each other and heat flows from the warmer to the cooler one. Skiers can lose body heat through conduction when their (warmer) skin touches (cooler) clothing or other objects. Scientists at California Institute of Technology explain:

> Conduction is the movement of heat through a substance by the collision of molecules. At the place where the two objects touch, the faster-moving molecules of the warmer object collide with the slower-moving molecules of the cooler object. As they collide, the faster molecules give up some of their energy to the slower molecules. . . . This process continues until heat energy from the warmer object spreads throughout the cooler object.[64]

Different objects conduct heat energy differently. Some, such as metals, are good conductors and transfer heat extremely well. This is why touching a hot metal pan can easily burn skin. Other substances, such as cloth, are not good conductors. In fact, holding a thick cloth, such as a potholder, that absorbs rather than transfers heat protects the hands from burns. Things that do not conduct heat efficiently are known as insulators. Wool, which traps air between its fibers, is a good insulator, so it helps slow down the travel of heat from a human body to the surrounding atmosphere. This is why many people wear wool in cold weather. The air between layers of clothing also provides good insula-

Surviving Hypothermia

The lower the body temperature goes in a hypothermic person, the less likely the chances of survival. Rarely, people whose core body temperature drops so much that they are clinically dead can be revived. In 1999, for example, twenty-nine-year-old Norwegian doctor Anna Bagenholm fell into an icy river while skiing. She remained in the water, trapped under ice for more than an hour while friends struggled to rescue her. Her body temperature dropped to 56.7°F (13.7°C) and her heart stopped.

On the helicopter ride to the hospital, medics performed CPR (cardiopulmonary resuscitation) to restart her heart, and at the hospital doctors performed a nine-hour procedure called a cardiopulmonary bypass. This procedure is similar to one used during heart surgery. In a bypass, a machine that acts like a heart and lungs circulates the patient's blood and breathes for the patient while the heart is not functioning. For people with hypothermia, the machine also rewarms the blood outside the body and puts the warm blood back inside. After the procedure, Bagenholm was on a ventilator for thirty-five days and in intensive care for two months, but she survived because she received CPR relatively soon after her body temperature dropped.

tion. According to the book *Understanding Physics: Motion, Sound and Heat*, "Wool and air are not warm in themselves, but give the effect of warmness by helping us conserve our own body heat."[65]

However, if clothing becomes wet from perspiration, rain, or snow, it loses most of its insulating properties, because water conducts heat better than air does. Heat from a wet skier is also transferred to the surrounding air by the process of convection. Heat transfer from convection usually occurs in gases and liquids when warmer areas of these gases or liquids rise, transferring heat to cooler areas. This can lead to rapid body heat loss when heat is transferred from warm body perspiration to cooler air circulating around a skier. In other words, when sweat evaporates, the body cools down quickly.

The other mechanism of heat transfer, radiation, occurs when objects or heat sources do not touch each other. For example, heat from the sun is transferred to people through electromagnetic radiation known as light. All objects and living creatures emit some radiation, and warmer objects give off more than cooler ones do. People in cold surroundings give off more radiant energy than objects around them, and these objects absorb the radiated energy. When people give off more radiant energy than they absorb, their body temperature drops.

Avalanches

Besides the danger of hypothermia, experts say the most dangerous cold-weather risk for skiers is an avalanche—a rushing torrent of snow that buries everything in its path. The United States Forest Service National Avalanche Center reports that thirty-four people died in avalanches in the United States between 2011 and 2012. "Avalanches come in many shapes and sizes and even small ones can be dangerous,"[66] the Forest Service states. Skiers can be buried alive and suffocate or freeze to death and can be battered with injuries if they live.

Avalanches usually occur on mountains with 30 to 45 degree inclines, but they can happen on other mountains as well. They tend to recur in the same places many times and

Rescuers help at the scene of a 2014 avalanche in Missoula, Montana. Avalanches are one of the greatest dangers that skiers face.

HOW SLAB AVALANCHES FORM

Changes in air temperature can result in an unstable layer of snow below the top layer. On a slopes steeper than 30 degrees, a trigger can cause the weak layer to collapse and the snowpack to avalanche. Triggers include strong winds, additional weight from more snow, and skiers.

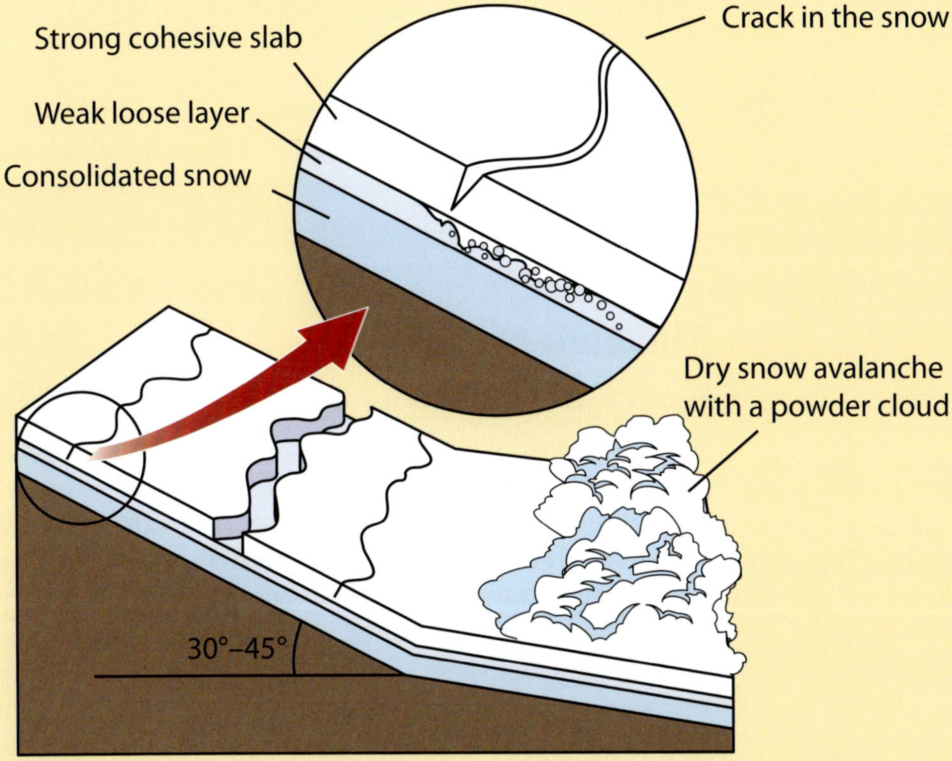

are often triggered by skiers skiing on unstable snowpacks. Sometimes avalanches can be prevented by bulldozing mountainsides or installing metal or concrete barriers, and sometimes ski patrols use explosives to launch manageable avalanches before a catastrophic one occurs naturally. However, this can also be dangerous. In December 2012, for example, the ski patrol at a Lake Tahoe ski resort triggered an intentional avalanche, and a ski patrolman named Bill Foster died when he was buried by snow.

Some skiers, particularly adventure skiers, now wear airbags to protect them if an avalanche occurs. In a February 2012 avalanche that killed three experienced skiers in Washington State, professional skier Elyse Saugstad managed to activate her airbag as she tumbled 3,000 feet (914m) down a mountainside. The airbag kept her head and arms above the snow and saved her life.

The Lure of Skiing

Despite the risks posed by avalanches, cold weather, falls, and collisions, skiing remains one of the most popular sports in the world. Scottish doctor Michael Langran, who specializes in skiing safety, states that this is partly because even though the risks of skiing are well-publicized, many skiers realize that the chances of dying are actually less than in many other sports. "In the U.S. during the past 10 years, about 41.5 people have died skiing/snowboarding per year on average. . . . Although it's not directly comparable, in the United States in 2009, 2,400 people drowned while swimming in public areas and 800 died while bicycle riding,"[67] Langran noted in a CNN article. He also points out that people who participate in sports such as football and soccer sustain many more injuries than those who ski.

For most people, however, choosing to ski has little to do with safety. In a discussion of why so many people like to ski, the Professional Ski Instructors of America website states, "For most, it's the exhilaration of spending time—alone or with friends—doing something that just makes you feel that much more alive."[68]

NOTES

Chapter 1: The History of Skiing

1. Roland Huntford. *Two Planks and a Passion*. London: Continuum, 2008, p. 2.
2. Holmenkollen Oslo Ski Museum. "Skiing History." www.holmenkollen.com/eng/The-Ski-Museum/Skiing-history.
3. David A. Lind and Scott P. Sanders. *The Physics of Skiing*, 2nd ed. New York: Springer-Verlag, 2013, pp. 2–3.
4. Sondre Norheim History. "Sondre in the History of Skiing." www.sondrenorheim.com/history.htm.
5. K. Lee Lerner and Brenda Wilmoth Lerner, eds. *World of Sports Science*. Detroit: Gale, 2007.
6. R.G. Lewis. "Learning to Ski." *Canadian Ski Year Book, 1935*. Canadian Ski Museum. www.skimuseum.ca/documents/annuals/1935-36_pt16_pg36-38.pdf.
7. Steve Hindman. *Cross-Country Skiing: Building Skills for Fun and Fitness*. Seattle: Mountaineers Books, 2010, p. 18.
8. Andrzej Peszek. *Ski Skills*. Buffalo, NY: Firefly Books, 2011, p. 18.
9. Peszek. *Ski Skills*, p. 6.

Chapter 2: Snow, Skis, and Skiers: The Physics of Skiing

10. Lind and Sanders. *The Physics of Skiing*, p. 12.
11. Mark Denny. *Gliding for Gold: The Physics of Winter Sports*. Baltimore: Johns Hopkins University Press, 2011, p. 14.
12. Gerald A. Smith. "Biomechanics of Cross Country Skiing," draft version of a chapter from *Handbook of Sports Medicine and Science: Cross Country Skiing*. http://biomekanikk.nih.no/xchandbook/index.html.
13. Denny. *Gliding for Gold*, p. 19.
14. Guy C. Warren, Samuel C. Colbeck, and Francis E. Kennedy. "Thermal Response of Downhill Skis." U.S. Army Corps of Engineers, Report 89-23, December 1989, p. 1.
15. Smith. "Biomechanics of Cross Country Skiing."

Chapter 3: Training a Skier's Body

16. Chris Fellows. *Total Skiing*. Champaign, IL: Human Kinetics, 2011, p. 25.

17. Sabine Krautgasser et al. "Physiological Responses of Elderly Recreational Alpine Skiers of Different Fitness and Skiing Abilities." *Journal of Sports Science and Medicine,* December 2011, p. 748.
18. Lerner and Lerner, eds. *World of Sports Science.*
19. James L. Moeller and Sami F. Rifat. *Winter Sports Medicine Handbook.* New York: McGraw-Hill, 2004, p. 16.
20. Jonathan F. Bean and Walter R. Frontera. "Strength and Power Training: A Guide for Adults of All Ages." Harvard Health Publications. www.harvardhealthcontent.com/HealthyLifestyle/70,SPT0313?Page=Section1.
21. Bean and Frontera. "Strength and Power Training."
22. Carl Petersen, Patricia Chuey, and Bob Morrell. "Fit to Ski—Nutritional Concerns." FIS Medical Committee Educational Series. https://assets.imgstg.com/assets/console/document/documents/nutrition-morrell.pdf.
23. Elena Diaz et al. "Cell Damage, Antioxidant Status, and Cortisol Levels Related to Nutrition in Ski Mountaineering During a Two-Day Race." *Journal of Sports Science and Medicine,* June 2010, p. 338.
24. Peszek. *Ski Skills,* p. 42.
25. Helen M. Binkley. "Strength, Size, or Power?" *NSCA's Performance Training Journal,* vol. 1, no. 4, p. 14.
26. Fellows. *Total Skiing,* p. 27.
27. David W. Bacharach, Ronald W. Kipp, and John G. Seifert. "The Effects of a Carbohydrate-Protein Gel Supplement on Alpine Slalom Ski Performance." *Journal of Sports Science and Medicine,* September 2012, p. 537.

Chapter 4: Courage and Other Mental Powers: Psychology and Skiing

28. Jim Taylor. "Inside the Ski Racing Mind: Demystifying Sport Psychology." *Ski Racing,* January 18, 2011. http://skiracing.com/?q=node/9217.
29. Jim Taylor. "Inside the Ski Racing Mind: Motivation to Succeed." *Ski Racing,* October 19, 2010. www.skiracing.com/?q=node/8914.
30. Chad Giese. "Discussion: A Great Essay on Motivation." *Attackpoint,* March 4, 2005. www.attackpoint.org/discussionthread.jsp/message_4093.
31. Quoted in Adam White. "Psychological Edge Separates MMU Alpine Skiers from the Pack." *Burlington Free Press,* December 19, 2012. www.usatodayhss.com/burlingtonfreepress/article/psychological-edge-separates-mmu-alpine-skiers-from-the-pack--2012312190006.
32. Quoted in E.G. Valens. *The Other Side of the Mountain.* New York: Harper & Row, 1966, pp. 99–100.
33. Quoted in Jeffrey Marlow. "How Science Turned a Struggling Pro

Skier into an Olympic Medal Contender." *Wired*, February 7, 2014, www.wired.com/2014/02/ski-run-nyman-sochi-olympics.

34. Quoted in Jason Wachob. "Olympic Q&A: Lindsey Vonn, USA Alpine Skiing." MindBody Green, February 9, 2010, www.mindbodygreen.com/0-317/Olympic-Q-A-Lindsey-Vonn-USA-Alpine-Skiing.html
35. Haley Perlus. "Race as Well as You Train—Ski Racing and Anxiety in Sports," *Podium Sports Journal*, January 7, 2011. www.podiumsportsjournal.com/2011/01/07/race-as-well-as-you-train-ski-racing-anxiety-in-sports.
36. Marvin Zuckerman. "Are You a Risk Taker?" *Psychology Today*, November 1, 2000. www.psychologytoday.com/articles/200011/are-you-risk-taker?page=3.
37. Steven Kotler. "The Addictive Nature of Adrenaline Sports." *Psychology Today*, March 15, 2008. www.psychologytoday.com/blog/the-playing-field/200803/the-addicitve-nature-adrenaline-sport.
38. Quoted in Bill Gifford. "Shane McConkey's Last Run." *Men's Journal*, July 2009. www.mensjournal.com/magazine/shane-mcconkeys-last-run-20131031?page=8.
39. Quoted in Wayne Drehs. "Being Roz G." X Games, January 25, 2013. http://xgames.espn.go.com/es-ES/skiing/article/8878293/roz-groenewoud-defend-title-women-ski-superpipe-x-games-aspen.

Chapter 5: Speed Matters: Downhill and Cross-Country Techniques

40. Peszek. *Ski Skills,* p. 59.
41. Valens. *The Other Side of the Mountain,* p. 63.
42. Canadian Ski Instructors Alliance. "Technique—The Canadian Approach." www.snowproab.com/skipro/pdfs/Physics_skiing_eng-2.pdf.
43. Denny. *Gliding for Gold,* p. 104.
44. Valens. *The Other Side of the Mountain,* p. 83.
45. Lind and Sanders. *The Physics of Skiing,* p. 71.
46. Bacharach, Kipp, and Seifert. "The effects of a carbohydrate-protein gel supplement," p. 537.
47. Lerner and Lerner, eds. *World of Sports Science,* p. 635.
48. Luis Manzano Benito et al. "An Analysis of Performance in Elite Young Cross-Country Skiing: Classical Style vs. Skate Skiing." *Journal of Social Science,* October 2011, p. 565.

Chapter 6: Jumps and Acrobatics: Ski Jumping and Freestyle Techniques

49. Janez Vodicar, Milan Coh, and Bojan Jost. "Kinematic Structure at the Early Flight Position in Ski Jumping." *Journal of Human Kinetics*, December 2012, vol. 35, p. 35.

50. John Gleaves. "Too Fit to Fly: How Female Nordic Ski Jumping Challenges the IOC's Approach to Gender Equality." *Proceedings: International Symposium for Olympic Research,* Annual 2010, p. 278.
51. Denny. *Gliding for Gold,* pp. 134–135.
52. B. Schmolzer and W. Muller. "Individual Flight Styles in Ski Jumping: Results Obtained During Olympic Games Competitions." *Journal of Biomechanics,* May 2005, vol. 38, p. 1055.
53. W. Muller. "Determinants of Ski-Jump Performance and Implications for Health, Safety, and Fairness." *Sports Medicine,* 2009, vol. 39, p. 85.
54. Donald P. Wylie. "Who Hits Harder: The Nordic Skier or Aerial Jumper?" NASA. http://pumas.gsfc.nasa.gov/files/05_10_99_1.pdf.
55. Freestyle Ski Acrobatique. "Aerials." http://freestyleski.com/wp/about/freestyle-101/disciplines.
56. Quoted in Deborah Williams. "Ski Moguls Like Moseley." *Ski,* March 26, 2012. www.skinet.com/ski/moseleymoguls.
57. Quoted in *USA Today*. "Canadian Freestyle Skier Sarah Burke Dies at 29," January 19, 2102. http://usatoday30.usatoday.com/sports/olympics/story/2012-01-19/freestyle-skier-sarah-burke-death/52680120/1.

Chapter 7: The Slippery Slope: Skiing Injuries

58. Moeller and Rifat. *Winter Sports Medicine Handbook,* p. xv.
59. Josef Kroll et al. "Changes in Quadriceps Muscle Activity During Sustained Recreational Alpine Skiing." *Journal of Sports Science and Medicine,* March 2011, p. 81.
60. Barbara Sibbald. "Yes to ski helmets, but buyer beware." *Canadian Medical Association Journal,* April 3, 2012, p. 627.
61. Quoted in Cathy Reid. "Thanks Coach! Alisa Camplin to Todd Ossian and Daniel Murphy." Australian Sports Commission. https://secure.ausport.gov.au/__data/assets/pdf_file/0019/293023/28405Reid.pdf.
62. Jacek Kruzel, Katarzyna Ogrodzka, and Tomasz Ridan. "Injuries of the Knee Joint in Chosen Winter Sports Disciplines." *Medicina Sportiva,* September 2011, p. 132.
63. Quoted in *Canadian Press*. "Alpine Canada Summit Examines Skiing Injuries," May 2, 2011. www.cbc.ca/sports/alpineskiing/story/2011/05/02/sp-ski-canada-safety-summit.html.
64. Cal Tech Cool Cosmos. "How Does Heat Travel?" http://coolcosmos.ipac.caltech.edu/cosmic_classroom/light_lessons/thermal/transfer.html.
65. Isaac Asimov. "Thermodynamics." *Understanding Physics: Motion, Sound and Heat.* http://mysite

.pratt.edu/~arch543p/readings/thermodynamics.html.

66. Forest Service National Avalanche Center. "Kinds of Avalanches." www.fsavalanche.org/Default.aspx?ContentId=4&LinkId=10&Parent-LinkId=9.
67. Quoted in Paul Gittings. "Danger on the Slopes: Are Winter Sports Safe?" CNN, January 14, 2013. http://edition.cnn.com/2013/01/14/sport/skiing-risks-deaths-injuries.
68. Professional Ski Instructors of America and American Association of Snowboard Instructors. "Why Ski or Snowboard?" www.thesnowpros.org/WhySkiingorSnowboardingisforYou/WhySkiorSnowboard.aspx.

GLOSSARY

adventure skiing: A hybrid between Alpine and Nordic skiing done in the backcountry.

aerials: A type of freestyle skiing that involves skiers jumping off a ramp and performing acrobatic tricks in the air.

aerodynamic drag: Air resistance that holds moving objects back.

agility: The ability to move quickly in any direction while maintaining balance.

Alpine skiing: Downhill skiing.

bindings: The parts of skis that anchor them to a skier's boots.

biomechanics: The study of how the principles of physics and mechanics apply to human motion.

camber: A quality of skis that makes them higher in the middle than at the ends.

centrifugal force: The force that causes something moving in a curve to be pushed away from the center of the curve.

centripetal force: The force that pulls something moving in a curve toward the center of the curve.

force: A push or pull on an object.

freestyle skiing: Types of skiing that include acrobatics.

friction: A force that slows the progress of an object.

inertia: The tendency of an object at rest to remain at rest.

kinetic: Moving.

ligament: Cartilage that connects bones to each other.

mass: The amount of matter an object contains.

moguls: Man-made bumps; a type of freestyle skiing that involves skiing down a steep hill filled with bumps while performing jumps and acrobatics.

momentum: The tendency of an object in motion to remain in motion.

neuron: A nerve cell.

neurotransmitter: A brain chemical that neurons use to communicate.

Nordic skiing: Cross-country skiing and other types that use free-heel ski bindings.

parabolic ski: A ski with sidecut edges that carve the shape of a parabola in the snow.

physics: The science that studies and explains the qualities and relationships between physical objects.

plyometrics: Power-building exercises that stretch a muscle group before contracting it.

power: The ability to exert strength quickly.

psychology: The science of the mind, or psyche.

ski lift: A device that transports skiers up a hill.

slalom: A type of downhill skiing where competitors skillfully maneuver around a series of gates.

sports medicine: The area of medicine devoted to studying, preventing, and treating sports injuries.

stability: The ability to maintain one's position when outside forces act to disrupt it.

tendon: Cartilage that connects muscles to bones.

velocity: A measurement of how fast an object is changing its original position.

FOR MORE INFORMATION

Books

Katrin Barth and Hubert Bruhl. *Training Cross-Country Skiing*. Germany: Meyer and Meyer Verlag, 2006. Written for teens about skiing basics, the book covers psychology, technique, and nutrition.

Ronald W. Kipp. *Alpine Skiing* (*Outdoor Adventures* Series). Champaign, IL: Human Kinetics, 2012. Aimed at teens and preteens, this book covers the history, equipment, training, skills, and techniques for Alpine skiing.

Internet Sources

"Going for the Glide." Norwegian University of Science and Technology, February 21, 2010. www.ntnu.edu/news/going-for-the-glide. This article explains how ski wax and environmental conditions affect Olympic skiers.

"Winter Sports Science." Sun-Sentinel News in Education. http://interactive.sun-sentinel.com/services/newspaper/education/nie/Wsports_layout.pdf. Explains the science of winter sports and offers activities that show how these aspects of science work.

Films

Downhill Science: Alpine Skiing (www.nbclearn.com/olympics/cuecard/47275). Olympic skiers and scientists discuss the science of downhill skiing in this 2009 video from NBC Learn.

Science of Skiing (www.bbc.co.uk/learningzone/clips/science-of-skiing/10856.html). Short video from the British Broadcasting Company with details about snow friction and how custom skis increase competitors' speed.

Science of the Winter Olympic Games: The Science of Skis (www.nsf.gov/news/special_reports/olympics/skis.jsp). In this video, scientists and Olympic athletes explain how the qualities of skis influence skiing speed.

INDEX

PICTURE CREDITS

Cover: © Val Thoermer/Shutterstock.com, © dolomite-summits/Shutterstock.com, © Irina Rogova/Shutterstock.com
© Aamir Qureshi/AFP/Getty Images, 40
© AFP/Getty Images, 14
© Alain Grosclaude/Agence Zoom/Getty Images, 36
© AP Photo/Dominic Favre/Keystone, 72
© AP Photo/Matthias Schrader, 61
© AP Photo/Peter Dejong, 100
© AP Photo/Scott Sady/Reno Sparks Convention and Visitor's Authority, 64
© AP Photo/Sergei Grits, 88
© AP Photo/Tom Bauer/The Missoulian, 106
© Branger/Roger Viollet/Getty Images, 19
© Brian Cassella/Chicago Tribune/MCT via Getty Images, 74
© Christof Koepsel/Getty Images for BMW, 77
© CORR/AFP/Getty Images, 16
© Dave Buston/AFP/Getty Images, 103
© David E. Klutho/Sports Illustrated/Getty Images, 91
© Don Emmert/AFP/Getty Images, 70
© Drew Gardner /Sports Illustrated/Getty Images, 48
© EyesWideOpen/Getty Images, 25
© Fabrice Coffrini/AFP/Getty Images, 34, 99
© Gale, Cengage Learning, 21, 30, 45, 82, 107
© Jean-Pierre Clatot/AFP/Getty Images, 93
© Jens Meyer/Associated Press, 32
© Kathryn Scott Osler/The Denver Post via Getty Images, 55
© Keystone-France/Gamma-Keystone via Getty Images, 11
© Matthew Stockman/Getty Images, 53
© Michael Kappeler/AFP/Getty Images, 44
© MyLoupe/UIG via Getty Images, 38
© Odd Andersen/AFP/Getty Images, 79
© Olivier Morin/AFP/Getty Images, 81
© Underwood Archives/Getty Images, 12

ABOUT THE AUTHOR

Melissa Abramovitz has been an author of educational books and magazine articles for more than twenty-five years. Many of her published works deal with science, nature, and health topics. She is also the author of both children's picture books and an acclaimed book for writers.